CW01496413

FUNDAMENTAL IMAGE

Sourabh Chatterji

Contents

Preface

After returning from the hospital, the irascible old Vijayant undergoes a curious transformation. He starts growing younger. Yet as his body regains its past strength and firmness, his mind continues to retain the acerbic perspicacity borne out of experience and age, allowing him a unique perspective to see the present from the eyes of the past. In this strange situation, gradually the barriers between the past and the present dissolve setting him on a surreal journey far into the deep to discover his original grief which had blanched the very fabric of his life.

A vague sense of a lack pervades within us all the time. Even in the moments of utmost happiness it sustains, rather, it makes its presence felt even more. What is the cause of this permanent pallor that colours the sky of our life? In fact, it is not the sky, it is our own eyes that have turned pale. Why? Because of the road we have travelled. Time did not just pass by us, it passed through us and in doing so left impressions on our minds that became a part of what we are and how we acted subsequently. But the past is not just the memories we have of it. Past comprises everything - the things that we remember and also the things we've forgotten. Most of the time it is these forgotten unimportant things, things so mundane that we abandon them to the far deep corners of the unconscious, that define us and our life. That is the soil that nurtures the roots of our existence. 'Fundamental Image' uncovers this aspect of the psyche through the surreal life of a resentful mind.

I apologise to the reader for the formatting errors that he might encounter along the way, but I assure him that these are only inadvertent mistakes of omission and not the result of haste or carelessness. I felt that I could not give the content to a professional editor for he might look at it with a conventional eye and miss out the nuances. For example, the direct speech in the story is enclosed within double quotes i.e., " ". These are the words that are spoken by the characters. But the thoughts are enclosed within single quotes i.e. ' '. This was necessary because a large part of the story comprises the inner monologue of the protagonist and there was a need to keep that distinction lest the reader confuse it with spoken words or the narrator's voice. Yet, despite my best and repeated efforts, I might have left out certain errors. I sincerely hope that the reader will ignore them with the generosity that concerns itself with the spirit rather than the form.

S.C
May 2024

Chapter One

He looked at the window.

'Still dark'.

He closed his eyes.

A bursting brilliance perforated his being. A silverbright vista opened. Cool bluish light, blow of the breeze, sway of the trees, smell of the leaves. Fresh full breath! Ah! This lone cloud stretches like a silver streak, infinite openness, profound peace!! Release! Dong!

Vijayant awoke startled. Yet he felt he hadn't slept at all. He was too weary to sit up. He turned his head towards the window again. A dull dusty ray streamed through the brown curtains momentarily illuminating the meaningless clamour of the insignificant particles before they were lost in the darkness again. A sickly warmth imbued the air with a sullen boredom. He raised his head from the pillow and looked between his feet. Wife's garlanded picture hung high on the wall, above the door. He dropped his head back. On the other side, a lonely old clock clacked on a blank chipped wall. He squinted his eyes to make out the time.

'Just six...That's it! Have been lying for so long! Does it matter?... What matters?' Grumbling and reluctant, he sat up on the bed. He was mostly grumbling and reluctant now.

A solitary old bed lay in the centre of a large square room. The walls had holes and nails, remnants of the painting or a picture that hung there once. Now empty, the off-white walls seemed bigger and the room seemed like a hall and the whole had a brown hue due to the dark brown curtains on the door and the windows. A plain yellow wall clock hung high on one wall. Below sat an old wooden chest. A small wall mounted TV held the space between them like an opening into a different time zone. Alongside the chest, a door opened into narrow closet that led to the bathroom. The wall opposite was supported by a chair and a study table whose one corner was held by an electric kettle. A tall bookshelf, stuffed with rare old books, suffocating with profundity, stood beside the study table overwatching the head of the bed from a side. On the other side of the study table was a dressing table with minimal paraphernalia like a comb and hair oil. Alongside was a window filtering in the dullness from the morning. An old picture of Vijayant's late wife hung on the front wall above the door. Opposite, beyond the head of the bed, was a wall sized window, curtained, that opened to the terrace that opened to the sky. Time had stripped off the room of everything that was else and filled it with an isolated emptiness.

'Where the hell! ... ', Vijayant's feet were trying to find his slippers . 'I took them down here so that I could find them when I wake up!...Damn!...Things just slip away! Why can't I hold them! They walked away themselves? Damn!'

Irritated red, he got up and bent his tall frame under the bed.

'I hate this! Everything comes up to the head!'

The slippers were further under the bed. He stood up straight wore the slippers and lumbered towards the bathroom. At eighty years he walked quite straight.

The door opened into a narrow dressing room with a built-in wardrobe on one side and wooden shelves on the other, on which old black military trunks were kept. He walked across and put on the light switch, and opened the bathroom door. The bright white light hurt his eyes. A frowning grimace looked back through the mirror. It looked horrible. He had a different image of himself in his mind. He immediately straightened his face and tried to wear a calmer look. 'A high nose begins to hang as you grow old and wrinkles are fairly visible on a fair clean-shaven skin. All this magnifies the frown,' He justified to himself rolling his hand over his head to settle down his hard grey hair. Baldness had not touched him yet.

An enlarged prostrate made the urination painfully difficult. He grunted and grumbled even more. 'All happiness boils down to health. No man can be happy if he is sick'. His mind kept chattering while he wrapped up his morning basics. 'In pain every moment is endless....In old age life boils down to the basics....realize too late that...that is all that is there to life.'

Cumbersomely he dressed up for his morning walk and came to the stairway and cursed, as usual, 'Son of a ...! Told him to put me up downstairs...but they want to send me up! Up, right up to hell!He thinks he is very wise...how will I go out if I can't go downstairs!' He stepped on the first step and then cursed at every step, 'At eighty I have to step down these stairs every day. Why couldn't he let me stay on the ground floor? Sons and daughters! Who would believe that these cute little flowers will grow up to be such...evil? Can't believe I taught him...' Then he cursed as he got down the final few steps, '...to walk, to speak, to read, to write, to think!! Huff!' He opened the door that led through the front yard to the gate. 'Now they don't even feel like our own. Just like someone else!... Separate! Different! Detached! We all are so... alone!'

There was some movement at the door behind and Sumeet came out.

"Papa! you are going?"

'Yodelling donkeylike from behind...bad omen!' Vijayant stopped and looked back with a frown.

"Papa the infection is spreading ... I told you that. The government is telling everyone to stay at home yet you keep going out for your walks every day. Don't you watch the news?"

"No, I don't! That's why I haven't gone mad like you all."

4

"It's serious come back! You have lung problem as it is." Sumeet came out and walked down a few steps.

"Mind your own business! If you were so worried about me you should have kept me downstairs."

"Again the same thing! ... You have more privacy and space there. Ground floor is thoroughfare. You have an attached store-bathroom. That's more important."

"Don't begin your day with excuses!"

'Attached bathroom! Of course! Detached people and attached bathrooms, that's modern life.'

Exasperated, Sumeet lumbered back.

No sooner did he open the gate than his eyes popped out with rage.

'A** h***s! Again, some monkey has parked right in front of the gate.'

He looked around. Nobody. It was early morning. He looked at the 'No Parking' board hung on the gate.

'Can't these tribals read this board! Does this even need to be told?'

Suddenly a middle-aged man in a grey uniform came running in awkwardly across from the other side of the road.

"Is that you Mr Democracy who parks whatever, wherever?"

The oleaginous man groveled, "Sarrysar, too much paapulation, too much cars, no space InIndiaa!"

5

"Therefore, you stole the space? By the way, there's all the space you want. It's empty in the morning. You could have parked somewhere else."

"Hurry sar! Buying medicine! Flu sar! Two minnut only sar! Don't get angry, you are our elder, I am taking out sar!"

"Just take out your taxi! I don't want to see it when I come back!"

'Bloody uncivilized civilians! So casual about others!' He walked away hurriedly tapping his stick on the pavement.

'This was outskirts... peaceful, open...now a market ahead... chock full ... people people people...swarms like worms... but we can't stop marrying and reproducing... that's the purpose and meaning of life.' He walked on grumbling, head bent, looking straight, looking down. Barely he looked up or around. Nothing interested him. There was nothing new to see. Nothing meant anything. They were just there. This was his daily circuit and he just wanted to be done with it. 'Smells like smoke... turned this green earth into grey ash...its stuffy, warm so early in the morning! Summer? Not yet!' Far away a faint rolling pitch of an Asian koel arose. His heart repelled instantly. 'Why do they cry so much in the morning... This sun will burn us up after some time...this country... Huh!' Tired and breathless he turned back.

"The pandemic is not over yet. At your age, you can't take such risks." Sumeet warned.

"What will happen? Will I die? As it is I am no less than dead!"

"It's serious. I don't know how you went out. Things are just beginning to open up after the shutdown."

Smita entered with a tray in her hand. Vijayant glared at her.

"Breakfast!" She said unfazed. She was used to those looks.

"Oats again! Great! That makes me feel reeeally healthy, and old! I really feel sick now... ... I won't have it!"

"Have a little bit Papa! You must have something."

"Thanks for your guidance wise man but one doesn't feel like eating when one feels like shitting."

"OK! Go then! Who's stopping you?"

"You!"

"Fine! I am going. Your breakfast is kept here."

"That's not breakfast! That's oats! invented by corporates so that these lazy fat ass women don't have to cook breakfast! Bloody corporate oats!"

Sumeet shook his head, looked at Smita and they both walked out.

Vijayant's eyes followed them out of the door. Stealthily he got up, went up to the door, looked downstairs to confirm their departure, and then furtively bolted the door. Then he walked up briskly to the study table, opened the drawer, and took out the packet of cigarettes.

The lighter was there in the pack itself. He took out a cigarette put it on the exact spot on his lips and lighted it in one click of the lighter. Unlike the reluctant fumbling laziness till now, there was focused promptness in the series of these actions. As he blew out the smoke his brows relaxed for the first time since he woke up.

"Thare you see! Smoking again!" Smita stopped cutting vegetables and looked up, "I told you he hasn't left it yet."

"Leave it, he is old, let him do whatever makes him happy." Sumeet said looking up. "As it is he is always sad and angry."

"But why? We take so much care... look after..."

"He has been like that forever...even before you came."

"He always snaps...should be a little understanding. He only told me to make light food in the morning...now he's throwing tantrums. He makes you feel... just worthless!"

"Don't expect kindness from him. We do the best we can. He is my father."

"And what about your brother... sitting comfortably in US even though he is older... should be taking the responsibility."

"Told you! Papa won't go to America. He won't budge. He is an army man."

"No longer! At his age, he has to be more mature."

"Huh! What's age got to do with maturity? Anyway when the body isn't functioning properly then the mind remains uneasy... Smita he is my father. I know how you feel... but... but you are mature!"

'Ah!' He blew out the smoke and relaxed on the WC. 'Relief means a good shit. Rest all is bull shit!'

He came back to his room. The water in the kettle was already boiling. He put the cup of green tea to brew picked up the rolled newspaper on the table and slammed it back on the table.

"Good morning mosquitoes!" Then he flipped the newspaper back on the table, drew back the curtain slightly, and walked out onto the terrace with a steaming cup of green tea.

Two young women, all decked up, walked up briskly towards the main road. His eyes followed them for a while but then he became conscious and looked the other way. He knew he was not enamoured by their glamour. There was something strange about them. They seemed weirdly garish and looked uncomfortable and stiff in their outfit. He contrasted his feelings with that of his youth. Then he would have found them attractive. But now! How the nature of feelings changes with the change in the body and how the inner world colours the outer.

'The world is how I am!'

He lit one more cigarette and floated away into a reverie with the smoke he blew out. Disorganized buildings and towers rose like a million greedy fingers of a concrete monster, clambering up to swallow up the sky. The earth trembled with the grumble of the descending aeroplanes and the sky reverberated with horn of the train. Soon mankind burst out from the peripheries and poured out into the streets like ants from their colonies. Clamouring vehicles rushed and jostled up with each other. Even before the sun could rise above the horizon the world came up, spread out, and swallowed up the space, the silence, the peace, the earth, the sky, the air. Vijayant was witnessing a disaster. He felt queasy and suddenly everything just blanked.

Chapter Two

"Papa! Papa! Get up!" Sumeet joggled his father. Vijayant lay drooling on the terrace. Smita stood behind Sumeet.

"Careful! he might be having the flu."

"So?... should I leave him here?"

"Listen, wear this mask, wear this poncho. The ambulance is on its way. Wait! Smita heard something and went up to the window I think it's here...It's here!"

Two paramedics all covered up in their personal protection gear stood outside the gate. Raising his hand one of them warned loudly, " Wait! Stay there! Maintain distance, what's the problem?"

"He is unconscious."

"Age?"

"Eighty."

"Ailment? Prior ailment?"

"Blood Pressure! high!"

One of them came up and placed an oxymeter on Vijayant's finger. He saw the reading and looked at his partner.

"Mr! Put him in the ambulance, sit with him and get yourself also tested for COVID", he said.

The middle-sized government hospital was a scene of horrifying pandemonium. Ambulances rushed blaring through the driveway overtaking one another to secure a spot under the porch, to disembark the patient. The entrance was swamped by the crowd jostling with the security who miserably failed to control them. It was impossible to get Vijayant inside. The paramedic thought for a moment, got down the stretcher from the ambulance and shouted

"Infected! move aside! You all will catch it and die!"

Flabbergasted the crowd dispersed and the patient was slid in through the gate. There was bedlam in the lobby inside. Breathless anxious patients were lying on the benches, chairs, floor or wherever they could find a place. All faces covered, all running helterskelter, it was difficult to make out a doctor from an attendant or a staff. Sumeet looked around for someone to guide him.

"Since when?" Two bespectacled owl eyes gaped from a slender short stature. A lady doctor had appeared from somewhere.

"Hun?" Sumeet was taken aback.

"Since when is he unconscious? How old?"

"Eighty... afternoon!"

"Oxygen?"

"The paramedic did not tell me."

She put a stethoscope on Vijayant's chest and then squinted her eyebrows slightly. Sumeet could see the clamour around but couldn't hear a breath. There was absolute silence as if he stood in a vacuum. The doctor shook her head.

"He is serious... I am telling you right now! ICU is full. Take him there... Room 39... I will come... Shankar! She called out at another staff passing thorough the corridor. She pointed her finger at Vijayant and said, Him... admission...ECG!" And then she vanished into the chaos.

Sumeet pushed the stretcher towards the ward.

"Bed eighteen." The staff indicated.

As they laid Vijayant on the bed Sumeet noticed that no patient in the ward was conscious.

"Do you arrange funerals?", Sumeet heard his voice resound in the lobby. As he spoke his eyes wandered around and found scared round eyes looking at him as if he was an undertaker. Perhaps he had spoken too loudly. Embarrassed he walked a little farther towards the corner and whispered into his mobile, "Yes...my father...Vijayant Singh... St Julian Hospital. Not Christian, Hindu... yes, a hearse is also required...electric crematorium will do... how can I tell you the time slot he is not dead yet!...How can I say when he will die?... What do you mean by package deal!... OK.... OK ... how much?... That's too much!... So now that funerals are in great demand you have raised the price!... Forty-eight thousand!!..I 'll get back!" Sumeet shook his head in disgust.

'People trying to make money out of your tragedy! Your crisis becomes someone's opportunity! That's the way with animals and that's the way with humans. Means and methods have changed but the instinct is the same. Civilization is animality with style!'

The doctor placed the stethoscope on Vijayant's chest again. Then she bent suddenly trying to hear harder.

"Sister Komila! Shankar! Where is the ECG? We need defibrillation, move to OT now! Fast!"

A white brilliance rose and pierced the sky. Blurred images floated across Vijayant's eyes. A lone cross wandered in the luminous sky.

The doctor called out as she pressed the defibrillator button again. "OK, I am clear! Everyone clear! Go!"

Leaves rustled lazily. A soothing warmth passed over his body. Giggles mingled with a twitter rose up like entwined coloured threads and burst into light blue sparkles resonating the vacancy.

Dr Anita performed CPR while the attendant prepared the injection.

The cloud tried to form but wind swept it away. He raised his hand to hold it together.

"One more! OK, I am clear, everyone clear! Go!"

A spark rose from his diaphragm and burst his eyes open. His chest rose high as he swallowed up all air he could.

"Mr Vijayant!" The nurse called out at the reception, "Who is here with Mr Vijayant Raj Singh!"

It was already midnight. Sumeet was dozing on a chair near the reception.

"Yes... Yes, that's... it's me!", Sumeet responded shaken up from his slumber.

"Yes! Ok wait here...Doctor will speak to you... maintain distance"

Sumeet was ready for the worst. By now he had adapted to the prevailing conditions. The pandemic was spreading rapidly and hundreds of deaths were being reported. Through the day he had seen many bodies pass by. His father had a slender chance. He felt a strange sense of release in his surrender to the circumstances. While others around him were anxious and scared, he waited there calmly watching the doctor walk up through the corridor in hurried short steps.

"Your father?"

Sumeet did not feel the need to confirm.

"We have shifted him to ICU."

"ICU? You mean he is not..." In a moment Sumeet jumped from depression to hyper anxiety, "How is he?"

"Respiratory shock."

"No, I'm fine!"

"No! Your father...he went into a respiratory shock."

Sumeet was confused. "Will he? ..."

"We are monitoring him." She did not have time for another question.

15

"He is alive!...Shhh..t....Sh..S...Still!" Smita whispered out with astonishment

"Yes." Sumeet answered blandly, still confused about how to react.

"Where is he now?"

"ICU."

"Is he conscious?"

"I don't know... I don't know! They are just rushing here and there. Nobody has time for anybody!!" Sumeet grew exasperated and disconnected the phone.

"Good morning, Mr Vijayant, how are you?"

"What do you think?" Vijayant was back to his insolent self.

"Well, you look incredible Mr Vijayant! It is incredible indeed!" Trying hard to hide her surprise the round-spectacled doctor looked at him like an owl. "Why have you made him sit?", she said looking at the nurse, "we can raise the bed for you if you want."

"No I'm alright", Vijayant raised his hand, " I sat up by myself."

In the middle of a pandemic, the ICU staff was not expecting a patient like Vijayant. They looked on at him ball-eyed and suspicious as if he was news of a disaster in a fine expensive envelope, a wave in retreat to lunge back as a tsunami.

"Asking for toast and omelet for breakfast." The nurse whispered her concern to the doctor.

"Oh! That's very good you are feeling hungry?" "Can you show me the vitals?" She whispered to the nurse.

"Nothing here." The nurse murmured handing over the clipboard.

"We would like to run some tests before you start taking normal food." The doctor said while going through the overnight record.

"How many of you are going to test me? How many times?" Vijayant sneered.

"Sir, we'll have to check. This kind of response is not normal."

"Get me out of this God damn sick place, can you? I am fine!"

"Shift him to a Medical 1 Komila! We will monitor him for twenty-four hours more. There are other serious patients in need of a bed here.

Sumeet peered through the glassed entrance. Vijayant was walking up through the central corridor. He wasn't carrying his walking stick. Yet his gait seemed quite firm. A staff with a dead body on a stretcher passed by him to the other side. Sumeet was dumbfounded. In the last forty-eight hours he had seen so many deaths, men and women much younger than his father, helpless, breathless surrendering to the relentless sweep of death. But his father! Colonel Vijayant Raj Singh had defeated death and was returning victorious with the usual defiant squint between his eyebrows looking even more formidable. 'What makes him so?', he wondered.

"Watch the steps!" Sumeet held out his hand.

"I am fine", Vijayant half raised his hand to say no.

Vijayant sat in the car easily without his help, Sumeet looked on amazed.

"You look so fresh you look like you're coming out of some massage parlour."

"Guess they took good care of me."

Vijayant walked inside briskly without acknowledging Smita. At the stairs, he hesitated, held the railings, and went up a few steps, let go of the railings, and then went up smoothly. Then he stood at the threshold and looked down. Both Sumeet and Smita were looking up at him, open-mouthed and wide-eyed as if a malevolent ghost hung over them. A nervous- pleasant shiver ran through him.

"How do you feel?" Sumeet sat on the bed near Vijayant's feet.

Feel? He contemplated as if exploring within, "I feel ...nothing... unusual"

"You asked Smita for tea? You haven't had tea for a while."

"Oh! it causes acidity but today I feel like having it. Tell Smita to give me something solid for breakfast. I feel hungry. Give me something like bread &omelet."

"OK! OK! You go freshen up, I'll get it. How do you breathe?"

"I am breathing fine."

'Five sentences. No acerbic remark!' Sumeet looked at his father deeply. With his age and health, even an ordinary fever should have worn him down. But he looked rather rejuvenated, reinvigorated! Sumeet looked at the watch. It was eleven A.M.

"You never slept so late for a long time."

Sumeet's questions were making Vijayant anxious and conscious yet he did not react. He was puzzled and was deeply examining himself. Sumeet also didn't want to wake up the irascible fire-vomiting dragon. He restrained himself and quietly left the room.

'How do I feel?' He felt nothing and it was great. For the first time in so many years, there was no pain anywhere and when there is no pain you feel nothing. The body just dissolves and what remains is just the mind. Mind! His mind was no longer compressed hot. It was...calm....getting calmer. 'Perplexing'.

He noticed that he had been sitting without support for about 15-20 minutes and there was no discomfort. He put down his legs to get into his slippers but his feet couldn't find them again. He got up from the bed and bent to locate the slippers. Suddenly he realized that he did not find bending cumbersome anymore. An unexpected blessing is treated more with disbelief than gratitude. In the age of reason, scepticism is the only wisdom.

Confused he walked up to the bathroom. The lights didn't hurt. He had no time to look at himself in the mirror and sat down on the WC immediately. As he began to ease, he realized that he had sat down without any support, and without a piercing pinch in his knees and back. As gas and stool released, deep in his gut he could feel the relief as the distension in his intestines relaxed. He felt freed from an eternal internal strangulation. And he had not even smoked!

He passed his hand over his stubbles. It seemed his wrinkles had lightened a bit. He shaved up hurriedly and examined his face further. Now even his eyes looked different- the skin around seemed to have smoothened a bit. The eyelids were not drooping and the white of the eye- it was firmer and whiter. He was not sure. Sumeet had made no remarks about them. He brushed and his gums did not hurt anymore. An idea occurred and he started filling up the bathtub immediately. Even if he was better for an hour, he wanted to take a good bath. Turning and bending had been so difficult and scared of drowning, he had not laid in the bathtub for ages. He took off his clothes and as he lifted his leg and raised his hand to hold on to something to enter, he realized that he was stable and did not need any support-'Incredible!' He said to himself. As he entered into the bathtub his excitement rose with the water till he laid. Then he floated up as if in paradise.

After a while, he sat up and began scrubbing himself softly. For so long he had not seen his body so deeply. Now it felt like a rare sculpture. He noticed the index finger of the right hand. It looked different. He washed off the foam and examined it again. It looked smooth. Lifting up his other arm, he placed both arms side by side. The index finger of the right hand was definitely smoother.

While wiping he inspected himself carefully again. There were one or two patches that he hadn't noticed before. One on his calf and one behind his thighs. But he was not sure. 'Who goes to find the grooves up his asshole', He thought. But he did notice that he could wipe himself off without any twitch or pain and that he had almost jumped out of the bathtub. Just to make sure he lifted his right arm and looked in the mirror once again. There it was. A patch of smoothness.

"Dad! Papa!"

Vijayant was startled!

"Are you done? Do you need me to wipe your legs?" Sumeet shouted from outside.

"Wait I'm done. I am coming." He spoke gravely.

'Plain simple answer!' Sumeet was surprised at not getting a rude retort. It felt strange.

Vijayant walked out of the bathroom wearing a towel. Sumeet noticed the firmness in his steps. He took the vest from the chair.

"Turn back"

"I am fine Sumeet! I'll do this myself. You haven't gone yet?"

"Where?"

"Office?"

"No ..."

"Let me wear this myself, I feel a little better today. I will get ready myself."

Sumeet looked dazed, "Your voice feels different!" He said

"Why? What happened ?"

"It's not that heavy. It isn't shaking."

"You go, let me get ready. I'll call you if I need something."

Sumeet turned back to leave. 'He is so calm and collected!' He could count on his fingers when he had seen him like this. 'Might be one of those days', he thought. He reached the door, thought something, and turned back.

"You remember them giving you something in the hospital."

"Of course!" Vijayant said while he combed his hair in the mirror.

What!", Sumeet turned completely.

"Peace."

Like a hungry predator, Vijayant secured his plate between his arms and chewed vigourously.

Men in slender health supplant their lack of appetite with deliberate and delicate manners. Here there was no such sophistication. Smita looked on amazed. She had never seen Vijayant in his prime. Suddenly Vijayant raised his eyes and spoke with his mouth full.

"Can I have another toast?"

Startled she rushed outside. When she returned Vijayant had already finished and was sitting with his back reclined against the chair.

"How many eggs?" He asked in a cold voice.

"Hun?"

"The omelet was made of how many eggs?"

"Two", she said.

"Make it four tomorrow onwards. What omeletRamoo Ram used to make! It is best that on Sunday one sits down for fifteen minutes and plans a good menu for the entire week, then buys all the stuff accordingly and makes the food as per the menu. It is simple! You just have to lay down 'procedures'."

Smita knew that compared to Vijayant's usual standards this was an extremely polite manner of actually saying 'You are worthless and stupid!'

She was so thankful she almost burst into tears.

Chapter Three

Someone was battering the door. Again, he had slept till late. Rays were bursting in inside. He looked at the watch. By now he would be returning from his walk. Annoyed with himself he got up, walked up and unbolted the door. Vijayant did not notice his smooth and swift movements. He was getting used to them. But he did notice that the maid standing at the door looked at him curiously.

Vijayant went back and pulled the window curtains aside, put on the TV and promptly changed to some channel playing Indian classical instrumental. The vibrations of the Tanpura reverberated in the emptiness. The housemaid stood bewildered following Vijayant's swift and purposeful movements.

Vijayant noticed her gazing.

"Wrap it up a little fast."

The moment Vijayant said that, he cautioned himself. He could not afford to be caustic with her. This was a typical urban, professional, housemaid : Overly and brightly dressed with a brilliant vermillion in the centre of her head declaring her marital status. Such colourful brightness in her society was a proof of youth, marriage and livelihood and she proclaimed her status with prideful embellishments. Even more, nature had compensated her for her height with curvaceous and full endowments. Blessed by circumstances and nature it was a privilege of this house that she had arrived today for the work for which she was paid for, for even one day of her absence meant everything was left to Smita which was as good as left. Stood in the centre of the room, a bright buxom bride with a bucket and a broom.

"Could you please, clean under the bed also...today."

She widened her eyes as if she'd been asked to donate her kidney.

"Please!" He pleaded and the generous woman relented, reluctantly.

Vijayant walked out into the terrace with a faint smile. He looked around for a while, his eyes wandering the blue sky bathed in light. In that lazy pleasant reverie he casually turned around. Inside the room he could see two full moon like protuberances moving, back and forth, under the bed. His wandering eyes began to gain focus. Then laser like, they pierced through the glass and travelling over all the undulations finally stumbled upon a pair of satin smooth breasts, needlessly covered, touch rubbing the floor...almost. Vijayant stood hypnotized, his vision floating back and forth in harmony with the movement. Suddenly the movement stopped. Abruptly the maid stood up, covered up her waist and chest with her saree and went towards the closet.

Mortified and irritated Vijayant cursed himself, 'Damn! What has happened to me?'

Just like a dog digs out the earth following some instinct, he dragged out one box after the other out of the closet. Himself. It was not driven by nostalgia. A strange energy rushed within him clamouring with a need unknown, like an unsated hunger. Now he stood in the centre with the black old trunks spread out around him. With a questioning look towards them he wondered what answers was he looking for. Randomly, he went up to one of them and opened it.

First were the albums, set neatly one beside the other like a fat layer over everything underneath. On them, in centre, lay an old paper, yellowed, folded half, alone. Memory of a deep pain arose and filled his chest. He picked up the paper and unfolded it. They were the impressions of soles of both feet, in Aalta (*Bengali, a red dye applied by Indian women, especially married women, to their hands and feet*). They were the last imprints of his mother's feet just before she was cremated.

"No."

"Why?"

Ashish and Suchitra sat on a simple authorized pattern sofa in the drawing room of the Army Officer's Bachelors Accommodation. It was a medium-sized two-room set. Furnished only with government authorized essentials, the room had a communist aura about it. Nothing had been purchased or added by Vijayant except a few personals. It also exemplified disinterestedness and detachment.

His parents had succeeded in finding Vijayant after tremendous efforts and were able to secure a meeting with him after a lot of persuasion. They looked sad, tired and grey. Both seemed to have aged rapidly. Abandonment by their only son showed on their face. Meanwhile, Vijayant stood at the window looking outside with his stern expression which rarely left his face now.

"I don't believe in marriage." Vijayant retorted.

"What nonsense!"....Suchitra's dismay exacerbated her ashened complexion. She thought for a moment and warned, "We will not be there for you always. After we are gone you would be absolutely alone."

Vijayant turned back aghast. His sneer turned into a villainous laughter.

"Now what is there to laugh?"

"Ha Ah! Of course with you and papa I never felt alone!" In a moment of brief silence his expression hardened and in a cursing challenging whisper he declared , "I was always alone, I am alone, I don't have any problem being alone. I won't feel alone after you are gone."

"Don't you love your mother?...Every mother wants to see her son married."

"Why? What have you got to do with my wife? When it came to supporting me then you turned your back but now you want a share of my present, control of my future!!"

"Show some respect....to your father."

"I can't! ...Why have you come here!"

"Because I am your mother!" Suchitra hollered and then started sobbing, "I am dying."

The clamour was replaced by silence. But Vijayant wasn't agitated. Rather his face hardened further, "What happened?"

"Breast cancer." She whispered as if she carried a curse. Her eyes were seeing death .

"Third stage." Ashish breathed out defeated.

He thought for a while and spoke, scornfully, "So, if I get married, are you going to survive?... Look at you, you want me to get married to this ugly oncologist so that your expenses are moderated and you are well looked after."

"No!" Suchitra stood up protesting loudly. "What are you even thinking! I met this nice girl in the hospital and I liked her. I want someone to look after you after I die."

Vijayant ambled around a while, ruminating, then he walked up to Suchitra and held her hands softly. Mustering every speckle of kindness from every corner of his heart, harnessing every micro drop of moisture in his eyes, drawing all the sympathy that could spring forth from his hoarse throat, he said, "Mom... .... everyone dies." Then suddenly he transcended into a realm of strange philosophical profundity and spoke unhindered without any consideration of the appropriateness of the occasion, "Why so much drama? There is life and then there is death! From the moment we are born we are running towards death. You are sad as if your death is going to be a terrible loss to the universe. Believe me it means nothing. I am much younger than you but I have seen death closely. Not even a leaf stops fluttering when you, me or anybody dies. No earth shatters, no sky breaks apart, no rain falls, no bird cries. So stop grieving about your death, it doesn't matter. When you are dying stare at death and laugh at it. That matters!"

He continued walking up and down the room pondering, reflecting and thinking aloud. "We have made such a villain of death! Imagine if there was no death. Not only your body but your wounds, your pain, your mistakes, your regrets, your loss! Everything would just live on. We would become a garbage truck. Garbage! Putrefying, stinking garbage of which you can never get rid of. You know in many countries they are researching on how to extend youth! How to extend life! Youth! Imagine living on this tsunamic wave of passions, ignorance, naivety', desire, anger, love and hate, forever for what? Sex: sex, sex sex all the time! ... Whole damn life! Those fools don't know that by extending life you don't renew it, you mummify it. Extending life is just an advanced form of mummification. That's it! Because...", he said stressing as if trying to explain it a child, "You need an end to begin again, to begin anew. When you are dead all your diseases, grievances, mistakes also die and nothing can hurt anymore. Death is a gift! You know! when Osho died his disciples sang and

29

danced and celebrated his death. That's what he wished them to do!!"

Ashish and Suchitra looked on aghast as if they were looking at a wandering ghost gone mad. Vijayant went on, "You think it is your motherly spirit that you want someone to take care of me after you are gone! No! Its your ego. You feel that you are so important that I will not survive without you. So you want your replica, your image to be around me after your death. You are projecting yourself on my would-be wife." He thought for a moment more and then said, "Life and immortality are incompatible. If you have to be immortal you have to cross this river of death. The realm of immortality starts beyond ....."

"Stop!! I'm not afraid of dying...I don't want to die because...."

"Because?" Vijayant's chain of thought had been interrupted ... "Because?"

"Because of your mental condition." Suchitra had tears in her eyes.

"What do you mean?"

"What do I mean! This mental condition of yours! Your madtalk." She thundered. "I don't want to send you to a mad-house. And after I die there should be someone to look after you and this girl is a doctor."

Vijayant was flabbergasted, "You think what I just said was madness?"

"I just want someone to look after you." Suchitra looked down apologetically.

"That's the problem! Truth seems madtalk to you."

"Your mother is dying and you?... Instead of sympathising with her you want her to go prancing around the garden holding a garland welcoming her own death?"

"I am not saying that ...huh! Such profound thoughts, if I would have been ancient Greece, people would call me a philosopher..."

"O to hell with your philosophy! There is no philosophy once you are dead you son of a... Socrates!"

Vijayant shook his head. Then something came to his mind and he smiled, "You know, you can even smoke now, as much as you want, what will they say, smoking causes cancer. Well, you already have cancer."

Now Ashish's patience gave way, "You are punishing us aren't you ?.... Just because we did not fund your medicine?"

"Well I am not punishing you, someone else is. Now she has cancer! May be If I would've been a doctor, you could at least have saved some money. By the way how much have you spent?...On her treatment... I am sure you both would have counted every penny of it."

"Yes of course! We counted because it's the blood of our body"

"How much is what I'm asking"

"About four lakhs (*Approximately $ 5000*)."

"Hah hahhah! By God sometimes I also feel that there is some God. But I am thankful to you indeed. You have taught me so much about selfishness. It helped me to get rid of this delusion of love of a mother and a father that they show in Hindi movies. Still, I won't get married. I don't need someone. I don't know if I will be able to live with someone or someone will be able to live with me... ...tell me one advantage of getting married, just one!", Vijayant said raising his right index finger.

"You will have sex! At least once!" Ashish blurted out excitedly. Suchitra smirked. Ashish tried to rationalise his statement, "Otherwise I don't think with your face and your grace you're ever going to get it!"

Vijayant fell back on the sofa, defeated.

Faint dreamy eyes hung over the imprints. The night was dead quiet. Vijayant and Ashish lifted her cautiously and lay her body on the floor. He had seen his mother writhing in pain. Now, every atom of her body had fallen silent, the spirit in every atom had left. Exorcised, she lay in peaceful gratitude. Vijayant glanced at his father. Ashish was breathing deeply, freed from the fear of 'what'llhappenif.' The worst was here and all that could be done was to face it.

On his palms, he felt the touch of her cold body, when he had laid her on the floor, and felt the warmth of her funeral pyre on his face. 'What time is it? Afternoon? Evening?' Everything seemed now. Past and present. Past in the present! He saw himself crying in the night when Suchitra had turned his back on him. What he needed was not MBBS (*Basic course in medicine to become a medical practitioner*) but just a caress of assurance, just a cuddle of acceptance. Suchitra had denied it to him. Then when Suchitra came for solace, he had denied her the same - equally. But isn't denial a kind of restraint. What did they both restrain from each other? Why weren't they able to face each other's grief?

His ramblings about the inevitability of death had been proven right. But, is being 'right' enough? Truth is much more than what is proved and what is right. As he had said, death was a gift. After the pain of cancer, indeed it was. But only to Suchitra. To him it was a loss and that day when his mother was crying she was indeed crying for him, for his loss. A tear dropped on the pale paper and smeared the red impressions.

He came out to the terrace to breathe. A plane passed by, quite low, and its steely whirring noise tunneled through his being. A breeze followed and a warm breath filled his chest. He looked up anxiously. The haze hung heavily. Yet one star fought its way through the gloom and met the grief song rising from his heart midway.

When I was young my mother told,
That stars are our loved ones,

33

But as I grew the world grew into me,
And I dismissed this as superstition.

I walked through life, hope and despair,
Through happiness and through sadness,
Whenever I looked up in the sky,
I found an accompanying brightness.

One night flashed through the mind,
A streak like no other,
That star is always there with me,
Since I lost my mother.

Chapter Four

He was reluctant to open the albums now. He just laid them outside, on the chest in ones and twos. Yet, as he picked up the last one, the thinnest, he couldn't stop himself from opening it. They were mostly photos of Sharon. First, there was a photo of their marriage reception. She was so remarkably beautiful! Tall and slender, yet her cheeks were just full and her smile was free. Any man would desire such a girl. Yet he felt distant from her. He turned over a few leafs. There was again a photo of Sharon sitting on a chair holding Vineet and Sumeet in her lap. But now she looked quite different. A graveness watched through her smiling face. She had matured. And then again, another one with him. He remembered getting it clicked when they had got back together again. She was a completely different person now, smiling proudly standing beside her sons who stood taller than her. She looked distant. Something struck him and he turned over to the first leaf again.

He wondered why he never noticed when she was alive. Sharon had grown sad over the years. Her eyes wore a shadow as if they had withdrawn, within. Her lips had dried. Memories arose as images and past events began to play in front of his eyes like a movie. But now he was not the actor but a witness, standing aside, watching. He never knew that moments could unlink from time, fall into the deep recesses of the mind and lie there for ages, until one day, stirred up by something, they would rise up to surface of consciousness and float in front of your eyes making you the only audience of your own drama and the only witness of your own truth.

"What happened?" Vijayant sat up. The bed was shaking."

"Something's biting me.", Sharon got down the bed rubbing the back of her shoulder.

"What is it?....must be an ant or something." He put on the bedside lamp. Sharon put on the main light.

"There is something... some needle!"

Vijayant scanned the bed.

"Is there something below the bedsheet?" She said.

He got down the bed and said, "Just let me...just remove this bedsheet and see. They both searched the particular place on the bed."

"See this!" She held it up to his face, "This is hurting me!"

"This!.. This is a hair... This is your hair... How can it hurt?"

"No! It hurts, see! it's red on my back."

Vijayant looked at the back of her shoulder, it was red as if bitten by an ant. "I can't believe this! How can someone be so.... I have only heard this in fairy tales...There must be something else!"

"No! it is this that hurts. I'm telling you!" Sharon protested.

"Faaiene! ...let's get back to sleep. I have to leave early morning."

As Vijayant came back smiling to his side of the bed he glanced at her. The sullenness of her innocent face settled in him as the souvenir of that night.

The grumbling of the descending plane pulled him out into the present. 'She was so tender!' Scenes from his own marriage rose up again. How she came carried on a chowki(A flat stool for sitting) lifted up by her brothers across the hall upto the altar and presented to him like a gift. How she giggled all the way thinking her face couldn't be seen through the veil. Yet he could not remember himself thinking anything else other than just getting over with it. He had heard his mother talk about her beauty and he thought...'So what!'

He came to the photo where she held Sumeet and Vineet in her lap. She looked distant, sitting on a chair, a little sideways, as if she had been looking at something else on the other side and suddenly the photographer had called them out and clicked the photo. Both Vineet and Sumeet sat on her lap looking at the camera as if they were surprised by the flash. But Sharon's smile was forced and her eyes were so dry. How harshly had he treated her but he understood nothing then.

"VJ! VJ!"

Vijayant could barely open his eyes. Sharon was bent upon him. Sumeet squalled incessantly.

"VJ can we go to the doctor? Both of us are not well Sumeet hasn't slept a wink." Her voice was hoarse with cold.

"It must be viral then!" He said petulantly "…. nothing serious go to sleep!"

"But he is not able to sleep!"

Vijayant sat up on the bed and said, "Give them some medicine from the drawer… In the morning you can go to the doctor."

"The medicines are finished… I know"

"Suffer then!" He yelled. "You know we have children in the house. We must always have medicines. Now at two in the morning, you suddenly remember that you don't have medicines?"

"But we have been having them, it didn't work!"

"I don't want to get into an argument in the middle of the night…" He shouted louder and was taken aback. Sharon sat on the bed sideways. There he saw - Sumeet sitting on her lap like a chubby fair doll. He wasn't crying anymore. Rather he was looking at him stunned, scared, guilty. Vineet had woken up, crawled up and went and sat beside Sumeet, also on her mother's lap. Both were looking at Vijayant as if he were an angry monster like they were looking at the camera. That's how they looked at him. Now he saw.

'Everything is mixed up', He couldn't take it anymore and tossed the album on the bed and walked up to the window. He closed his eyes and let out a deep breath. The smogged-up, heavy, starless night still hung outside like a curse. A photo had slipped out of the album and lay on the bed alone.

"We have a party in the mess today. All ladies have to come."

"I can't."

"Why?"

"Because I am tired." She turned back to leave.

"Its an official function. Attendance of lady wives is mandatory."

"I can't go VJ, you go please, I want some relief, just want to sleep for an hour or so and I will be able to go on tomorrow."

"Why are you always tired! Other women also have children! They are around everywhere, but you are always just tired! Tired!" Vijayant stomped out of the room.

'Now they will ask about Sharon. 'Oooo! Where is she? Whaaayy! isnt she well?...Then they'll look deeply with suspicious eyes trying to dig out something exciting to gossip....It.s so embarrassing to lie all the time. Why is it even necessary to call these lazies in such social evenings? We can make do without them...so easily!' Baleful anxiety plagued him as he walked up into the Officers' Mess.

"Oh, there you are! Vijayant !" A colleague came up with open arms.

'There you go! Mr Breaking News. Now he will ask 'you came alone?'

"You came alone? Where is Sharon? I hope all well"

The insinuation was too sharp and true to hold Vijayant's patience, "You aren't even married! Hope all well?"

He had spoken so loudly, everyone noticed.

'Embarrassing bloody jokers', Vijayant walked up to the bar, "Large Rum and a pack of cigarettes!"

Vijayant opened the door, put on the light and said in a firm voice, "Just come outside."

Sharon took five minutes to come out. By that time Vijayant was already gurgling with anger. The moment he saw her he flew into a monstrous rage–"You liar!!! you deliberately did not go. You wanted to humiliate me in front of my colleagues. You think I don't know your tricks!"

"VJ I am not well! Seriously!" She pleaded. "There is just a one-year gap between these boys and I am finding it difficult to manage."

"And I am finding it difficult to manage this embarrassment!" He breathed out hard once, twice trying to calm himself, panting in his pungent stale breath filled with smoke and rum, like a smouldering monster seeking revenge. Then a hoarse heavy voice resounded the drawing room, "See! if you go back to your parents...I mean in Bangalore, they will certainly help you in bringing up these kids. At least I can say that my wife has gone to look after her old parents."

Sharon stood dumbstruck.

"I will get the tickets, as early as possible. Then you can go and rest, as much as you want."

"Shot! That's gone far!", Said the colleague of the other night. "Not yet lost the touch!"

Following the flight of the golf ball Vijayant smiled proudly. Then he looked around absorbing the pleasant morning on the golf course. Suddenly his mobile rang, he looked at the phone and his face grew grim. "Hello!" He spoke in a deep hard voice, "The train has left ? good!"

"All good?" The colleague following him asked.

"Everything is fine! Don't be nervous all the time," he turned back and walked on, alone.

Why did he turn away? From his mother, his father, his wife? What he had feared had happened. He had opened up a pandora's box of unanswered questions and unresolved emotions. And now they lay before him like festering wounds. That's why he had swept all the old baggage away. That's why he was reluctant to open the albums. Each memory was a leaf on the tree of his life. Each having its own place, shape, size and flavor, beauty, love! Yet, in their veins ran a darkness drawn up from some depth unknown and spread out across their fabric, like a patch of disease.

No sea soothed the heart.

Chapter Five

"Jai Hind Sir!" (*Victory to India: The normal salutation in the Indian Army*). Yuvraj whispered as he didn't want to shockwake his Company Commander, that too in a Counter Insurgency(CI) area. His young mellow voice was too soft to wake up Vijayant. "Jai Hind Saaar!" He whispered again stretching his shivering voice.

Vijayant woke up startled with wide open eyes and immediately sat up on the bed, "Five already?'

"Sir", Yuvraj replied regretfully. "Sir,tea", he held forth the glass in his shivering soft hands.

"Has it started snowing or what? Why is it so cold suddenly?"

"Must have snowed in the higher reaches sir."

"OK! Tell the Senior JCO (*Junior Commissioned Officer*) to meet me at zero six hundred and ask if all the parties are back."

"Sir, all parties are back." Yuvraj replied promptly. His slender figure was curled up on haunches preparing Vijayant's battle gear. Had it not been for his uniform someone would have mistaken him for a child.

"What about my packs for the patrol?"

"Yes sir...ready!" His innocent eyes shone brightly.

Vijayant nodded with squinted eyebrows, "Tell them to pack my breakfast. I'll have it on the way."

Yuvraj had been there with him for barely a fortnight. As he went about his chores Vijayantobserved him and wondered how can a person be so 'spotless'.

"Jai hind sir!", An old dour JCO stood on the door.

"Is the patrol party ready Sahab?" (*Sahab is the polite way of addressing an officer or JCO in the Indian Army*)

"One JCO and twelve Other Ranks on parade Sir." The old JCO replied in his usual weary manner. In the Counter Insurgency area this morning patrol was a routine unless there was an operation.

The orange rays of the sun swept up upon the sleeping deodars like a wave and the whole valley awakened to the resounding chirpings of the numerous songbirds. The whole scene was a sleeping Goddess awaking. Unbothered and undeviated by the phantasms of nature Vijayant led his patrol up the track moving up towards the sun with a soldier's single mindedness. On a flat feature they took a break.

"This is village?" Vijayant's asked indicating the hutments at the edge of the cliff.

"Sir SingoriGoti!" The soldier indicated on the map. Having climbed the steep slope the soldier gasped heavily unable to keep the map steady making it difficult for Vijayant to concentrate. Irritated easily, Vijayant moved away, looked around the horizon and walked upto the edge of the cliff to survey the valley below.

A little while later he turned back and said, "OK, we will move after fifteen. Don't forget to put a guard Manohar Sahab."

Manohar Sahab nodded and started passing the instructions. Vijayant went towards one side of the flat feature and started adjusting his gear. Other soldiers found a flat place and sat down to have breakfast. A young soldier put some eatables on a plate, went up to Vijayant and offered it. Vijayant looked at the food and took the plate reluctantly. Two guards stood on a higher ground watching over the area. They couldn't take a chance. These mountains were infested with the most violent insurgent groups. While the troops chatted with each other Vijayant stood aloof on one side waiting for them to finish, looking around.

The deodars rose up in rows, one after the other, up the slope, right up to the horizon. Beyond, rose the sun. The valley lay half awake and from its wet glistening green and orange bed, fog rose like breath, whispering something faintly and then melting into the sky. Nearby, he could hear the babbling of a stream intermingling with twittering of songbirds. From some unknown depth, a lone longing pitch of a plaintive cuckoo rose like an arrow and pierced through the valley. Far away from the chimney rose the smoke of a homely earth. In the face of such beauty all rationality crumbles, all doubts disintegrate and from the depths of the being arises a prayerful hymn in gratitude to an unknown, which is only known to the temple within. As if he awoke into a dream.

"Sahab! .... Sahab!... Sahab!"

A shiver ran down Vijayant's spine. His heart thumped. 'Criticality' Something whispered within. Recoiled sharply from his reverie he reproved himself for losing his alertness, still remaining straight-faced. Everyone looked on startled ready to take positions. Yuvraj was running up the slope gasping, with a satchel dangling in his hands.

"What happened? Manohar shouted back. Standoff attack on the post?"

Hearing the question Yuvraj abruptly halted his climb and replied with a shocked expression, "No Sahab!"

"Then why are you yelling like a snake bit your arse?"

"VJ Sahab! Breakfast... forgot to take it." He took out the tiffin from his satchel, looked at Vijayant and smiled faintly.

The entire patrol party smiled and looked at the Company Commander. "Don't worry we won't let your officer go hungry", Manohar Sahab said smiling.

Yet, Vijayant looked on straightfaced gazing into some emptiness. As Yuvraj walked up closer to hand over the breakfast Vijayant's face gradually contorted and then suddenly, he exploded.

"Breakfaaaast! You came here to give me breakfast! What will happen if I don't have breakfast for one day? Even if you had to come you should have come with a buddy... At least you should have carried your weapon... ...are you a civilian? You are soldier!!! And this is sensitive area infested with insurgents with people here sympathising with them and you are just sauntering around like you are a tourist... you fool! ...You could have been ambushed and killed...then inquiry will be held against me and I will be held responsible for not adhering to procedures and your death will be blamed upon me ...bloody chap!"

Then he charged up to Yuvraj, snatched the breakfast out of his hand and threw it.

"Nonsense! How old are you! Stupid fool!"

There was total silence. Aware of his terrible rage other troops looked the other way.

"I said how old!!", Vijayant growled.

"19 years old sir." Yuvraj whispered. All his excitement had vanished and he stood in a guilty attention- his head hung, shoulders dropped.

"19 Years!" You can elect a government so you can understand what is the security situation here."

Shaken Yuvraj saluted tentatively and turned back.

"Where are you going now?"

"To the company sir"

"Without a weapon! Alone! No you won't. You'll accompany us"

47

"In those canvas shoes?" A soldier whispered.

"Complete non-military untrained, so called, soldiers! Don't know what garbage they send from the training centres these days" Vijayant cursed. "Sahab! the village down below... the ridge and this flat feature from the top...from there, click some photos ...and click one photo of the our patrol party also... Join up and carry something!" He bellowed at Yuvraj.

The night spread out infinite, like an overarching dark dispassionate force over the faint innocent light flickering on the mountainside, imploring to stay alive. Vijayant stood at the window of his cottage staring into the darkness. Suddenly he noticed a shadow fluttering at the corner of his eyes. Yuvraj sat on a campstool under a light alone with one leg on the other slowly pulling off the socks over his feet. The socks stuck to his feet soaked dry with blood. As he pulled the sock down slowly the skin peeled off and the blisters shone with all their gory gruesomeness. The young soldier grimaced through the painful ordeal as he suffocated his cries and drank up his tears silently. As the socks came down his blistering wounds, a scorching remorse ran up Vijayant's spine.

"Yes come in." Yuvraj came inside limping holding a shaking cup of tea. "Keep it there and sit down... show me your feet."

"SSSir...it's all right."

"Let me see...please!"

Yuvraj didn't expect such a mellow voice spring forth from such a coarse rough personality. He relented. Vijayant got down on his knees and inspected the wound closely.

"You washed it?"

"Yes sir."

Then he got up and went to the shelf, picked up a cream, came back sat on his haunches and started applying the cream on each of the blisters one by one.

"You have to understand the nuances Yuvraj. If I would have taken it lightly then the men would say that there are separate set of rules for officers and men. You don't understand it sends a signal that officer is careless. He forgot his breakfast when he has ordered every one else to be self-contained till evening. Now he wants a chap to deliver his breakfast even at the peril of his life. You could have called me on the radio."

"Sir we are poor people from the village. I only thought that you would go hungry. That's what my mother does, and that's what I did."

Vijayant raised his head looked at Yuvraj. Purged by pain, he sat there radiating a sublime innocence. No one had shown Vijayant this bare minimum compassion ever. Gratitude oozed out from the dry broken crevasses of his heart and moistened his eyes. Suddenly, embarrassed by their own humanity they shook away from each other.

"You…You take this cream… Rest for some time."

Yuvraj limped out of the room without saying a word.

Vijayant stood looking at the limping soldier departing. Thoughts and emotions crashed against each other while he remained in a state of suspended animation. As the soldier walked away a sense of embarrassment arose and started drawing closer. He had exposed his emotions. It was weakness. He tried hard to compensate himself. After a while he walked up to the magneto. A firm voice broke out of his throat. "Sahab, henceforth when we go for patrols some new soldiers should also accompany. They need to be trained."

"All ready?" Vijayant stood in the middle of a hollow square of soldiers in full gear.

"Yes sir!"

"Ok close up everyone." Vijayant laid out the map on the table beside. "Everyone can see? OK. There has been contact by Delta company at this location, Village Hirani. At about 0300 hours. Move of militants has been reported on the boundary of the forest over here." Vijayant indicated the locations on the map with the torch. Team leaders noted down the information in their notebooks. Navigators marked their maps. "Manohar Sahab! You will take the column from… note down…here, here and here. I will take the column from here and here. He waited a moment for Manohar to note the details. "Roger?"

"Roger Sahab!"

"You will go by vehicle in this direction and then get down and then move to your destination cross country from here. Any doubts?"

"Sahab GL(*Grenade Launcher*) has to be taken? What about mortar?" One NCO questioned.

"GL will be taken. The mortar at the Battalion Headquarters will be able to support us....Anything else?... Now hurry up and move now!" As Vijayant adjusted his gear and was about to leave something came to his mind. "Sahab!"

The gruff Senior JCO turned back and looked at him

"Is Yuvraj going?"

"No Sahab."

"He will come. You tell him to be my buddy and manage the radio."

The Senior JCO kept looking at Vijayant for a while. It was his way of expressing his doubts. Then he said, "OK Sahab!"

The evening had already set in. The sun had set behind the ridge. In the darkening stillness of the forest only the crackling of the dry leaves under the feet could be heard around. Vijayant's column had clambered up the steep hillside slowly and heavily and was closing up to the top when-trrrattrrrattrrrrat trat Boom trrattrrattrrat Boom!

Suddenly, intense machine gun fire came upon his column with hand grenades being simultaneously thrown upon the leading elements.

The party dashed and went to the ground immediately. Vijayant, Yuvraj and another soldier took cover behind a boulder. Suddenly, the firing stopped. Vijayant crawled up and from the corner of the boulder peered and tried to locate the direction from where the firing came. Then he curled back and indicated Yuvraj to come up.

"Mike over!... Mike over!...Mike Over!" Vijayant spoke on the radio carried by Yuvraj.

"Buzz...Buzzzz...", Came the reply on the radio. Manohar sahab was out of communication due to screening by the mountains.

Vijayant looked at other soldiers of his column and then spoke on the handheld radio "Victor 200 mtrs west the fire is coming from that barn!"

"Roger Sahab!"

"Victor 1 you provide cover fire, I will close up to the barn!"

The support group started firing and under the covering fire. Vijayant and Yuvraj moved up closer to the barn.

"Mike over!...Mike over!..." Vijayant again called up Manohar Sahab on the radio.

"Mbuzzzzzz....OKzzzzzzz!"

"Mike your strength is barely one! Mike I am just 100 mtrs south of the barn. Roger so far?"

"Gerzzzzzzz "

"Mike report your location?"

"Mikezzzzzzz location buzz, buzz zzzz."

"Mike nothing heard! Mike Send RL(*Rocket Launcher*) Det to my location. Press radio switch once if message clear!"

"Buzzzz!"

Vijayant and Yuvraj waited in the dead ground while random firing continued. Vijayant was cordoning the barn readjusting his detachments passing orders on the handheld radio. Suddenly he looked behind at the ridge across. He could see silouhettes of two men with RL moving along the ridge, completely in the field of fire of the terrorists hiding in the barn on this side. Mortal danger!

Vijayant wanted to shout but he stopped himself. That would give away his position.

"Mike over!... Mike over!...Mike over!... Mike over! Romeo... Romeo...Romeo over!" Vijayant whispered fervently on the radio. Yet there was no reply.

"Yuvraj! rush off to that RL party and divert them and tell them to take the detour and come from the other side."

"Right sir" Saying this Yuvraj crawled to one side and indicated to another soldier to come with him

"I cannot send another man in the middle of combat. You go alone and divert them!"

Yuvraj began to crawl away.

"Wait! How will I talk to Manohar if you take the radio?" He thought for a while and then said, "You leave the radio here and just carry your handheld ... ...reach there somehow and ...warn them and...Stay there!"

Yuvraj nodded and vanished into the darkness.

Intermittent firing continued throughout the night. After a while the RL party fetched up followed by Manohar Sahab an hour later. The barn was further cordoned off by columns from other companies. In the wee hours of the morning a full-fledged fire assault was launched upon the barn. Bodies of two terrorists were recovered. Finally, the mopping up started and the entire ridgeline was combed to flush out any remaining terrorists. Vijayant was overseeing the operation. Suddenly the blank mush of the radio was interrupted by a call.

"Delta for Victor over!"

"Victor for Delta pass your message!" Vijayant responded.

"Delta for Victor own casualty... one."

Vijayant felt a thud in his heart. The radio went silent. Vijayant couldn't even hear the mush. Gathering himself he called "Delta say again! "

"Delta for Victor...own casualty...one, fatal sir!"

"Victor for Delta Identify casualty!"

"Sir ... buzz...sir...buzz ..."

"Victor for Delta who is the casualty?"

"Rifleman Yuvraj Singh." The voice on the radio was hopeless. "Sir, the bullet went through his neck."

"Location?"

"Sir we are on the ridge! Sir one of us is raising his hand! Can you see across?"

Vijayant stood at the terrace window gazing into the gaping darkness outside, face flushed, eyes wide, barely breathing, holding a framed photo close to his chest. It was the photo of the patrol party clicked on the flat feature that day. Slowly, hesitantly he looked down, at the photograph. Yuvraj stood in the corner, in canvas shoes, embarrassed, tentative, flickering as if pleading to live. He turned back and walked up to the chest and kept the photograph. Painfully, carefully-The way Yuvraj pulled down his socks. The photo had peeled down the congealed layers of time over his wounds.

Yet, he couldn't tell anyone. He couldn't tell anyone of the moment of deep connection he had spent with Yuvraj. He couldn't tell anyone that he had taken him for the operation to train him to fight so that he could live, and not to get him killed. He couldn't tell anyone about his loss, he couldn't tell anyone about his grief, he couldn't tell anyone about his remorse. He couldn't because, he was a man, he was an officer, he couldn't be weak, he couldn't tell, share, grieve!

So he cut out that part of himself called humanness, and cremated it with Yuvraj. Yet the wounded whole from which that humanness was cut away lay festering under the layers of time, poisoning his soul. He felt a volcano gurgling in his chest and his stomach contorted with disgust. A deep anguish burst within but couldn't escape and just melted into his throat.

Chapter Six

There was a gradient in the youthfulness that moved from his feet upwards. Vijayant stood naked in the bathroom surveying his body. The feet looked firm and smooth but as he moved up the freshness gradually waned till it completely disappeared around his torso. He wondered if this was some skin disease. 'Should I consult the doctor?' Then he looked at himself again. How straight his posture had become! Suddenly he looked inside his underwear. Satisfaction swept his face. He introspected further : How did he feel?. He felt better than ever. 'I'm not going to the doctor', he concluded, 'Will take it as it comes. I've nothing to lose, I am already eighty' He came closer to the shaving mirror and examined his face carefully. 'Is this going to come right up to the face? Then everyone will know!'

"Who is it?", He came upto the door furtively and whispered. He had walked out of the bathroom naked.

"Thank God you are alive!...Breakfast!" Smita cried from the other side.

Flustered he rushed to the closet and wore a gown. As he walked back to the door he consciously adjusted his gait so as not to surprise his daughter-in-law.

Smita had a questioning look on her face, "I got worried! what took you so long?"

"Age." Vijayant replied plainly as he tried to look busy with something else.

"But yesterday you were quite swift!"

"Then I ate your breakfast." The retort was deliberate. He didn't want her to ask too many questions. He himself didn't have all the answers.

Smita was embarrassed as expected, "Why have you closed the door then. Keep it open as before, and why are all these items lying all.."

"What have you made?"

"Bread – Omlet... I thought you would be able to have it still." She said doubtfully as if reproaching herself for thinking that the old man will have the same appetite today also.

"Present the Omlette please, let me see."Vijayant responded confidently. He took the plate and moved swiftly to the study table, picked up a slip of paper and held it out to her. "Fine, now this is the menu, this food shall be cooked for me this week."

Smita looked at the slip then she looked lost and then she looked at Vijayant.

"Buy these items from the market accordingly and the food will be served at eight thirty, thirteen thirty and twenty thirty hours. Dot. Got it ?"

Smita was so flustered and astonished that she just forgot to mention anything about all the old boxes lying around the room. Vijayant stood straight right in the middle of the room in an old grey gown like Mandrake, the magician. Before she could react Vijayant, in his typical military manner, asserted

"Thank you... for your service...es."

Coming down the stairs Smita wondered at the firmness and the smoothness of Vijayant's demeanour. This, she hadn't experienced ever.

As Vijayant bolted the door from inside he heaved a sigh of relief and smiled. He was able to divert his daughter-in-law and maintain his secret. He walked back to the chest where he had spread out the items from the boxes. Inadvertently his eyes fell inside one of the boxes. Down under, it lay there. The mood swung immediately.

"Jai Hind Sir! Alpha squadron, Posted, One hundred Nine cadets, Present, One hundred and four cadets." The SCC (*Squadron Cadet Captain*) hesitated while giving the report to the instructor.

"Who all are missing?" The straight-faced instructor asked in a rough voice.

"Sir, one cadet has not finished yet, four are bringing him up." The SCC explained

"Who?"

"Sir Cadet Vijayant."

"Run! Come on run! its near! its right there, we've reached! See! See!" Cried a course mate who had already finished his run and had come back a few hundred yards to pull Vijayant to finish faster. Another senior who had come along mocked, "Hey see I am almost walking and you are still slower than me!" "Such a loser!" Another cursed, "This is his condition in the practice run! What will happen on the final day?"

"Don't worry, they will come last like hockey", Cadet Sachin smirked.

The Squadron was practicing cross country, preparing for the most prestigious event in the Academy scheduled next week - The Inter Squadron Cross Country Championship. Cross Country was the proof of mettle of a squadron in the Academy, so much so that even coming second was an achievement. Unlike other events, where selected participants were fielded, this was an event in which every cadet of a squadron participated and consequently everyone's performance mattered. A lapse by one would relegate the entire squadron down the ranking table. Rather, this was the ethos in the Academy. In almost every matter the entire squadron would suffer for the lapse of one. Therefore, it was important for a cadet to spare no effort to preclude such a predicament as shame for himself and more than that his squadron because of his own doing or undoing. The group mattered more than the individual. On the other hand, this also ensured that those who lagged behind, for any reason whatsoever, were carried along by the group. This was to build team spirit. Here Vijayant lagged behind. Being more habituated towards cerebral efforts from childhood, his body could not cope up easily with the physical demands of military life. In any physical activity whether it was PT, drill or sports his handicap was evident. He was failing his physical tests repeatedly and soon began to be seen as 'weak type'. In the closed society of men vying for the military uniform, where physical capability was the most important measure of a 'man', this incapability meant 'shame' for himself and his squadron. This also meant that he was a burden others had to carry, a support that did not always come forth willingly. Reproached by his instructors, mocked by his seniors and avoided by his batch mates the young and confident Vijayant curled up within himself like a venomous snake and lay smouldering.

As he limped up to the finishing enclosure, across the ground he could see the entire squadron looking back at him as if reflecting his embarrassment. After scorning Vijayant for his lack of commitment, the Divisional Officer (*Instructor*) dispersed the company. The Cadets rushed back to their squadron, few of them whining and complaining for being late and losing their Sunday.

"Let's rush, we already got late because someone just wanted to take it easy", Someone taunted.

"Thanks for teaching us patience Shaggo!" Sachin whispered in Vijayant's ears and jogged away giggling.

Vijayant stood there with shivering legs till everyone left. Then he dropped on his exhausted knees. With difficulty, he sat down and slowly and painfully pulled out his shoes. His feet emerged with socks soaked in blood. As he pulled down the socks the congealed layer of blood over his blisters came off and they shone with gory gruesomeness. He could not bear to see them. As the sun set on the horizon, he sat there seething in the scorching pain. Crying could have relieved him but it was shameful. Yet he could not stop the tears rolling down his cheeks. Perhaps, it was less from the scalding pain and more from a sense of being forsaken. He looked up and sighed 'Oh God! What is my mistake? I'm trying so hard!' No solace came from anywhere and his cry was lost in the grey emptiness of the sky. Helplessness intensified his grief and hiding his face in his palms he broke down, sobbing, 'Even You have forsaken me!'

Crying was relieving indeed. A balm on the scalded soul. He raised his head and wiped his tears. On the horizon, the dusk was dying in the arms of the night. A weariness swept over him also and he put his head over his knees and closed his eyes. It was relaxing to be away from the relentless hustle of society. Suddenly he felt a susurration on his back. Startled, he turned and saw a scrawny little puppy smelling him and wagging his tail. In normal circumstances, he would have shooed him away. But suffering had gifted him empathy. He could identify with the abandonment of that scraggy little mongrel. He swept his palm, wet with his own tears, softly over its bony head. The dog looked up with a surprised gratitude. Vijayant felt healed.

Raga Jansammohini on bansuri (*Wooden flute*) played on the tape recorder. Vijayant lay on his bed blankly staring at the ceiling. As the slow and peaceful tone of the bansuri seeped through his ears, his despondent pain dissolved into its soothing vibrations and adsorbed on his soul. He had been advised bed rest by the doctor due to his wounds. His roommate's bed laid against the opposite wall was empty. He had gone for training. This was a single room with a store and an attached bathroom which accommodated two cadets. Apart from the bed, there were two study tables placed at the feet of each bed facing opposite each other. Suddenly the door blasted open. ACA (Academy Cadet Adjutant) Aninder Pal Singh barged into the room.

"Bed rest?"

"Yes sir."

"Smart boy! Enjoying music eh? Gala time! Now do some work. I have to make this project. The topic is ...is ...wha' tha..." He couldn't recollect the name of his own project, "Yeah I remember! Indo- China War -1962. This is the stationary and this is some study material that I gathered after an hour of extensive research. All you have to do is find some more material, patch it up with this and prepare a nice-looking project for me. See! I have already done most of the work for you! Shouldn't be much of a problem since you are free. You just have to find some more material, that's it."

"Find some material from where? ... Sir." Vijayant was agitated. His senior had completely overlooked his injury and the fact that he was on bed rest on medical advice.

"Don't raise your voice!" The senior admonished Vijayant, "Just because I am frank with you doesn't mean that you can take me for granted. You better get this file ready by tomorrow evening for sure buddy, otherwise you watch... And listen you puss!", he looked at him abhorrently, "Everybody gets hurt once in a while. What's the big deal! Be mentally strong!"

'And you have to be morally strong!' Vijayant thought of retorting but restrained himself. He had already violated the norm by raising his voice. Talking back to a senior was totally unacceptable and would have caused trouble for his entire squadron batch.

"What are you drawing shammer?" Vijayant was startled. He was so immersed in his sketch that he didn't come to know when Sachin had sneaked into the room. "Wow, a woman! You're having a great time in training, isn't it? Music, women, and what not! That's what life is! You're one smart ass hole I tell you! Ya! Haahaa!" Suddenly he snatched the paper and vamoosed into the corridor, "Hey look at this! While we sweat like pigs, the maestro is finishing up his great work of art." While Sachin kept mocking him Vijayant followed limping behind with his arms stretched asking his sketch back. Other cadets in the corridor looked on, some smiled, and some sneered.

"I want to learn how to sham like him. After all, I also need rest." After running a little further suddenly Sachin turned back and said gravely, "Report to Divisional Officer's office immediately. Your Divo is looking for you."

'Now what have I done, I am on bed rest!', Exasperated he turned and trudged awkwardly towards the Squadron office.

"Jai hind sir, may I come in sir!" Vijayant stood at the threshold of the office.

"Wait!" Came a cold hard response from inside.

Vijayant limped back a bit and waited. It was quiet. Standing there he looked around. It was an old barrack with a double pitched roof that had been turned into a series of adjacent offices. There was a corridor that ran along its entire length. In front, there was a graveled open area where he was standing. Inadvertently his eyes wandered up to the evening sky. A lone kite, its wings spread full, floated high above. He felt a spark inside his head.

'Hold on! No matter what no one can stop time, tomorrow will come and so will the day after tomorrow, and one day this will get over and you will walk out of the gates with an assured salary. Then you have to depend on no fu****g body...for life–just hold on a little longer!' He breathed in a new resolve and felt the freedom of that kite in his own chest. Suddenly he heard the phone ring in the office.

"Cadet Vijayant! Come in."

"Vijayant walked inside the office and saluted. The straight-faced instructor raised the tele handset towards Vijayant, "Your father."

Vijayant's stomach contracted with anxiety but he managed to hide his feelings.

"You can speak to him. I'll be back", the instructor stood up and walked out.

"Hello! Hello! Vicky! Vicky!" Vijayant could hear his father's desperate voice on the other side. He waited for the instructor to leave, looked at the handset, kept it back on the phone, and walked out of the office.

"Okay! Listen up!", the straight-faced instructor wasn't as straight-faced today. "As you can see the weather is nice, the time is right and the best part-it's Sunday! So why not have some fun! Today we are going for a short ten kilometre practice run." The Divisional officer announced gaily. "And we are going to have a friendly...", he stressed the word, "competition with the Charleeees! Whichever squan wins will have midterm mood for two days!" He announced raising his two fingers "I know I know you are excited but let those Charleees fetch up first." He scoffed in his heavy voice.

"Those crunchies should not come ahead of us at any cost. The SCC was charging up the squadron. We need to plan! We are going to divide us into groups. Let's keep the good runners ahead and the best runners behind, and you shaggos you will be in the centre. And you! You will be in the absolute centre." He said pointing at Vijayant. Others giggled.

Everybody seemed quite excited about the proposal. But somehow Vijayant couldn't bring himself to feel excited about it. It was totally absurd, 'Someone makes you run for ten kilometres by screwing your Sunday so that there are no punishments on Monday...and Tuesday? Why so much animosity with Charlie Squadron! Why scoff at them? Aren't they the same army!' Then he saw the Charlie squadron jogging up to the ground equally excited and charged up and Vijayant started doubting himself.

"Chaaaaaarrrrrrrrrrleeeeeeeeeeeeeeees!" His squadron shouted challenging their rivals.

After mocking, jeering and challenging each other, the squadrons finally fell in at the start line. Everyone stood as if he was willing to lay down his life for the cause. Then with the word 'Go' the squadrons burst forth beyond the start line. Everyone pleaded, cheered, cursed and urged their mates to race ahead.

"Hey keep it! Don't you bloody change the pace." The SCC warned Vijayant

"I need space!" Vijayant shouted back

"Shut up! everyone is running!" The SCC rebuked panting heavily.

Vijayant ignored the SCC and started slowing down and maneuvering out of the group.

"Hey! Where are you going!"

But Vijayant had already exited the group and was now running parallel to it.

"If you fall back then watch out!" The SCC threatened.

By then Vijayant had already begun to disappear amongst others. Soon the nice and sunny Sunday turned into a rainy one. The squadron wise runners broke up into smaller groups of same pace runners, all splashing in the mud, sweating, rubbing and egging each other. Vijayant ran independently.

"OK gentlemen! the last 200 meters! Close in! Close in! Speed up! Speed up!" The Divisional officer cheered the cadets as they rushed into the enclosures.

Vijayant closed in into the third enclosure. It was considered more than 'respectable' and for him especially, it was a significant improvement. From the second enclosure, the SCC looked at him, astonished. Then he nodded to express his satisfaction. Vijayant looked at him and then looked away.

"Three cheers for Charleeess Hip hip hurray! hip hip hurray! hip hip hurray!" Alpha Squadron had won the 'friendly competition'. The cadets came back to the squadron cheering and celebrating. A dog wet from the rain had taken shelter in the corridor and sat shivering outside Vijayant's room. Shooed by the cadets leading the procession it whimpered.

"That's my room! Let him wait there!" Vijayant's firm voice echoed in the corridor. Startled the cadets looked back at him and walked away, leaving the dog alone.

"But sir I am not a boxer!"

"You will be, after this competition!" Said the SCC and started to walk away. Suddenly he turned back and came up to Vijayant stomping, "Every coursemate of yours has represented the squadron in at least one inter-squadron event, except you! Who are you? A spectator? This is the last event of the term. Can't you represent the squadron even in one event? Are you afraid of getting hurt? Bloody chap! gear up and go and sit on that bench and be ready for your bout!"

Vijayant could hear other cadets snigger. He went up and sat on the bench where other participants were sitting. After sometime a group of cadets from Charlie squadron came up and sat on the adjacent bench. They vigourously jabbered amongst themselves sharing their stratagems for the upcoming bout. Suddenly Vijayant heard a whisper.

"Shammer! Have you pissed in your pants already?"

Sachin, sitting on the next bench, was mocking him. Others in his group giggled along.

"OK pay attention everyone!" The referee walked up, "The first three bouts of this league will be as follows: -

Cadet Vijayant, A Squadron Vs Cadet Sachin, C Squadron. Your's is the first bout

Cadet Mubarak, A Squadron and Cadet Balkaran, B Squadron. Second and,

Cadet Manoj, A Squadron and Cadet Sanders, C Squadron. Third bout! Any doubts?"

Sachin made a V sign towards his eyes and pointed towards Vijayant in a gesture of challenge.

Vijayant thought for a moment and whispered into his mate's ears who sat nervously beside him, "How do you score points... You know how to play?"

"No! but this is not some play. You'll get humped if you don't fight."

"What do you do then?"

"Just put him down."

Both Vijayant and Sachin stood facing each other. The referee stood in between and spoke some instructions making vigourous gestures. Vijayant couldn't barely make out anything. Meanwhile, Sachin stared at him trying to get inside his eyes. Apparently, this was some psychological manipulation to dominate the opponent. Yet, Vijayant remained indifferent to the whole drama. He looked down at the floor of the ring as if examining it carefully. It wasn't that soft also. He was in the ring for the first time.

Charlie Squadron supporters thought Vijayant was nervous and they jeered. Sachin walked back to his corner with a confident sneer. Vijayant's squadron tried to match-up and cheered up their reluctant fighter.

The moment the referee waved his hand down Sachin sprung and threw a blow in flight. But Vijayant was a little farther and it only glanced his face. Even though tolerable, it hurt. What hurt more was the crowd jeering immediately after. Then Sachin went on a relentless offensive and kept throwing blow after blow. Vijayant kept taking a step back haphazardly. His random unconventional movements were making it difficult for Sachin to predict his next position and land an effective blow. He missed his punches again and again and started to tire out. Meanwhile, Vijayant kept slipping out like a cat. Suddenly Sachin got lucky and landed a full punch on Vijayant's cheekbone and the entire crowd broke into a tumultuous roar. It was a hard hit. Vijayant stood stunned. Suspecting something amiss the crowd dropped silent, the referee froze astounded, Sachin gazed confounded. A moment later Vijayant twitched and the entire crowd breathed out a sigh. But before anyone could gather himself a solid hit landed on Sachin's temple. Before he could regain his senses relentless blows started landing upon his entire body. The blows were being fired at such a rapid rate that he couldn't even release his breath and started to suffocate. He could hear screams from the crowd and the referee screaming Stop! Stop! Whistle No! No! Suddenly Sachin caught a glance of a cruel expressionless face and then felt an extraordinary pressure on his legs and chest. Then he heard a loud whistle, felt levitated, came and banged hard against the floor. An arrow pierced through his back and the sky vanished.

"Good afternoon,Ladies and Gentlemen! I welcome you all to the convocation ceremony of the Ninety-fifth course." A Cadet stood on the podium compeering the proceedings. "Today you will receive your Bachelor's Degrees in Science, Computer Science, and Arts. This occasion marks the successful culmination of an important phase in the training of the cadets of the passing out course. Now I would request the Chief Guest to award the medals and trophies to the meritorious cadets."

Best in PT, Cadet Shivraj Singh

Best in drill, Cadet Vilas Mohanrao Gaikwad

...and so the announcement went on and one by one the cadets marched up to the stage and accepted their prizes. Vijayant sat in the rear rows ruminating while others besides him sat half dozing being too tired from training to apply their mind to anything else. Suddenly the voice filtered through the applause and came and landed a thump on Vijayant's chest, "Best Project- Academy Cadet Adjutant Aninder Pal Singh!"

As Aninder Pal passed by him, through the alley, Vijayant felt his own face grow warm and wet. Aninder straightened up as he rose the stairs, marched up to the Commandant stiffly and accepted the award with the demeanour of a great scholar.

As the cadets started walk out of the auditorium, Vijayant, still standing in the alley, turned back and saw Aninder engaged in a banter with his mates. Suddenly he looked at Vijayant and started walking towards him. Vijayant stood still with an anticipative look on his face. Even though Aninder got all the accolades, expecting at least a cordial acknowledgment of his contribution from him was not something too much to ask for, he thought. Aninder came up and just passed by without even acknowledging his presence and went and vigorously shook hands with one of his coursemates on the other side. Vijayant began to leave.

"VJ!"

Vijayant turned back. The SCC came up to him and whispered. "You are being marched up tomorrow. Heckle order, nine hundred hours, Adjutant's office." He uttered the instructions with a sombre expression, without meeting his eyes and left immediately. The auditorium had already emptied out. For a while, Vijayant stood there staring into the hollowness and then walked away.

"Do you have to say anything, Cadet Vijayant Singh?"

At one end of the huge arched hall the Commandant of the Academy sat alone at the centre of a huge antique mahogany table. Three officer instructors stood on one side of the table, adjacent and equidistant from each other. On their opposite side stood the SCC, the referee and Sachin wearing a plaster on his hand and visibly bruised and swollen. Vijayant stood at the mouth of this hollow square. The cold baritone voice of the Commandant reverberated in the emptiness. Vijayant felt the crowd jeering at him with such vehemence as if, given an opportunity, they would tear away every layer of his being and rejoice drinking the blood from the pieces. A shiver ran down his ribs. He gathered his breath and uttered in an inconsistent voice.

"No, sir!"

"Relegated by six months, March him out!" The Commandant roared.

Sachin was waiting at the door. Vijayant walked up and unlocked his room without looking at him.

"Can I speak to you... for a moment?" Standing at the threshold, Sachin asked. Vijayant

74

was reluctant but he gave in. Sachin limped up to the study chair and sat down.

"You are terribly angry!" Sachin spoke in an unusually calm voice.

"I am not angry anymore."

"No, you are not angry with me! You are angry about something... you don't know."

Vijayant was intrigued. He looked at Sachin. He looked incredibly different now. The scorn that always lined his face was no longer there. Rather his face glowed with a childlike innocence as if he had been bathed free of any contempt for him. Vijayant's eyebrows puckered with a question. Sachin continued.

"That day when I hit you on the temple and you stood stunned...you remember?... I felt it stirred up a poison very deep within you."

Vijayant smirked, "Don't be too smug. You challenged me and I hammered you. That's the whole story. You had been misbehaving with me for quite some time. I don't know why? I have got my revenge and also the punishment for it. Its OK and you thought...."

Sachin stared at him so deeply that Vijayant felt awkward. Then he said, "Vijayant I am no professional boxer but I have been boxing since college. Losing and winning aside I know how to avoid at least two out of ten blows." Then he looked down as if introspecting deeply within and said, "We never know what demons hide inside us."

"One solid blow and its the demon inside you that has been exorcised. I hope now you are treated Sach. Why you used to mock me?"

"Sachin thought for a moment and said, "You know sitting in the hospital I wondered why I despised you so much...and I felt that in your sketches, in your attitude, in your stubbornness and even in your failures... ..."

Vijayant did not look at him, deliberately. It was the natural reluctance to hear the truth. Beneath Vijayant's outwardly defiance churned an unbearable anxiety.

"You held on to yourself while me, I lost myself...... in the crowd...and I felt bad about it."

Both sat silent, lost within. Violence had calmed the dislike they had for each other.

After a while Vijayant spoke, "You are also getting relegated ...medically?"

"No! I am being boarded out. Not fit to serve anymore."

Vijayant was stunned. He glanced at him from head to feet. "But you only fractured your hand!".

"There is an implant inside, plus my rib in the back also fractured that day." Sachin looked into his eyes scouring for a grain of kindness. But there was hardly any change in Vijayant's grave expression.

"Don't worry I told the Squadron Commander that I had misbehaved with you. That's why you just got relegated, otherwise you were also being boarded out...on account of discipline and that would have foreshadowed you throughout your life you know? Don't worry", he said again, "As it is I am not liking it much here. My parents never wanted me to join. We are a business family and I am the only son and all that you know? More than that I want to be loved...I mean be with my loved ones. You can have success with discipline... ... but life is much more than success." Then he waited for a moment, "Can I have my things back?"

"Your things?"

"Yeah, my stationery and pens and all. That Aninder gave to you for his project... didn't he?...Those water colours and pens, paints and drawing material. I also like to sketch and paint. That day he came asking for it. I won't have given it, because I didn't believe him but he told me he had to give it to you for a project. I saw you sketching many times...so..."

Vijayant got up opened the drawer of his study and took out the material, "I didn't know they were yours. But there is a problem..."

Sachin gave a questioning look.

"I can't find one of them. I have been looking for it. But I think I've lost it."

"Don't worry. If you find it, keep it as a souvenir. It will remind you of me. He chuckled as he got up to leave."

"Do you think I want to remember any of this?"

Vijayant smiled. He was holding the sketch pen in front of him. He opened it and drew a line on a piece of paper. It was a colourless scar. The ink had dried. He wondered what it meant to be lost then and to be found now. Or probably it was never lost. It just lay there unnoticed. How could something so insignificant and non-essential survive time when everything else, which seemed much more important, had perished along the way. But now that he had found it he wondered how much of his past it contained and how much of his present it coloured.

Chapter Seven

"MBBS!"

The lean middle-aged man sitting on the old two-seater netted chair snapped. He held a transistor in his hand from which a coarse buzz blared continually pouring noise into the already stuffed middle sized room. Rather, the room was small. There was not enough space to even lay a double bed. Therefore, two single beds were laid against the two adjacent walls at right angles to each other with the corner space between the two occupied by a table which was used for all purposes from studying to dining. The two-seater sat against the third wall. The walls were plain with old bright blue paint chipping off at places. A small gold foil image of Lord Hanuman hung on the wall above the two-seater and a mask of Durga hung at the centre of the wall opposite, above one of the beds. There were no curtains on the windows or the door which had to be kept open to reduce the suffocation inside. The yellow light from the bulb gave a dull bilious hue to the room which was further exacerbated by the shadow of the dangling old ceiling fan that made a metallic noise as it rotated tenuously. Books and newspapers lay piled up on a cemented shelf on wall above the table. The room and the ambience therein, exemplified the living conditions of a typical lower middle class Indian family of the late eighties repressed and inhibited by financial constraints. An adolescent and agitated Vijayant stood awkwardly in front of Ashish.

"So after MBBS what? Will you get a government job after that?"

"Can't be sure of a government job...I will most likely get a job in a private hospital... but...but I will be able to earn my living! One has to do MS, Doctor of Surgery or MD, Doctor of Medicine that is, to land up in a good job or practice independently." Vijayant tried to explain.

"And what do you have to do to become an MS or an MD?"

"You have to do MBBS."

"You mean after you do MBBS you will get admission to some MS or MD course, is it?"

"Not automatically. I'll have to appear for the competition again and get selected."

"And then you become a government doctor?"

"Well!" Vijayant was growing exasperated. "Then I will have to look for a vacancy in a government hospital or give a competition once again."

"And if you don't get selected then?"

"Then I'll try for a private hospital or put up a private clinic."

"And how much does MBBS cost?"

"It's around four-five lakhs(*$7000 Approx*) for complete MBBS."

"And for all this, you want coaching now?" Ashish spoke with a sarcastic smile on his face.

"Yes, because the competition is quite tough." Vijayant said trying to restrain his irritation, "Coaching increases the chances of success."

"And how much will coaching cost?"

"About 50,000 rupees (*$800 Approx*)."

Ashish smirked and said caustically, "And even after spending four-five lakhs you'll need more money to do MS and thereafter also... nothing is assured!"

"But I'll start earning even after MBBS!" Vijayant pleaded.

"How much!" Ashish snapped again, "Everything is so tentative... ...temporary! Firstly, what is the guarantee that you will qualify for MBBS at all? It's not all that easy and going by your results, highly unlikely. And even if you qualify nothing is guaranteed in the end. Do you see any logic?"

"But being a doctor!"

"Stop talking nonsense. We don't have the luxury of all this. Just get a good permanent, government job. Why not spend your time in preparing for something that you are more likely to succeed in and which will get you a salary directly rather than spending millions and still remaining unsure about qualification or income?"

"Papa everyone who has to become a doctor goes through the same rut! Have you ever seen a doctor not able to earn a living? Rather it is one of the most assured means of earning a living! I can be a doctor; I can take a student loan. I just need some support."

"Have you even seen your result? How have you done in the twelfth board? Lately, you have been quite indifferent to your studies. Tomorrow you are not able to complete MBBS then I'll end up paying the loan, I won't be your guarantor."

Vijayant felt a thud in his chest. He did not expect such a callous answer. He looked at his mother. A lean woman, she stood blankly with sunken eyes leaning on the kitchen door. Sweating with agitation he threw in his last plea.

"I always wanted to be a doctor. I have been preparing for it for quite some time."

"Doesn't look like you were preparing. Your performance has been continuously deteriorating over the last year and you tell me you were preparing! I cannot keep funding you throughout your life with nothing assured in the end. We are middle-class people I will not be able to handle such a financial adventure. We are teaching you so that you can bring money home not drain it away."

"Papa I was a ranker at one time! Give me a chance! Ritesh also got just sixty-three percent and he has been admitted to coaching by his father!" Vijayant scowled with frustration.

"That's because Ritesh's father is a fool! Look for a government job as I said, maybe a clerk. That's what seems possible."

"So that I can bring in the money as soon as possible, isn't it? That's all that matters!!" With his eyes teared up he stomped out of the room.

The noisy fan was hardly able to tackle the warm humid night. Vijayant lay sweating brooding on the bed. His father's carefree snore arising from the other bed frustrated him further. Suchitra came in tiptoeing and slid in beside Vijayant.

"Vicky! You haven't slept till now? It's late! College tomorrow."

"Why can't I do MBBS?" Vijayant brooded as he lay on the bed looking at the face mask of Durga just above him.

"Because we don't have the money." It was a deliberate expressionless expression.

"But Ma! we are not poor. We are middle class. We can manage somehow, can't we?"

"Shhh! Quiet! With your result, your father won't risk that kind of money...upon you." The last two words slipped out of her mouth inadvertently, yet they pierced his heart. Then she said looking into some emptiness, "We have to save for the future also Vicky! Face the facts !"

"But what about my future?" Vijayant turned his head towards his mother. His eyes pierced through the darkness. There was silence. No assurance came from the other side. Suddenly Suchitra turned to the other side and after a while started breathing deeply.

Riding his bicycle back from the college, a little further up the traffic signal, where he crossed the main street, there was a roadside bookstall. It was marked with advertisements for vacancies and competitions. Copies of 'Employment News' were placed on the stand immediately outside. He had noticed the stall previously but then it didn't matter. But today as he approached the signal, he had made up his mind already.

With chapped lips, Vijayant stood at the traffic signal withering in the dazzling summer sun. The loo conjured up ghosts of dust and debris that floated and whirled on the asphalt till they sighed and died. The dryness outside resonated with the barrenness inside. Yet the world carried on as usual, unbothered, incognizant, indifferent to his pain. Something dried up and shrivelled inside. His eyes squinted and a mild frown grew on his face. This was to become, gradually, his permanent facial expression, an outward representation of the resentment within.

He picked up the 'Employment News' and turned a few pages. The vendor looked anxious for his money.

"How much?" He asked

"Five rupees."

He thought for a moment, then he took out some coins from his bag and gave them to the shopkeeper. The shopkeeper eased and shifted to another customer. Vijayant opened his bag and carefully placed the Employment News between his books and rode back home.

Standing under the dull yellow light he keenly flipped through the pages of the newspaper scanning through the various advertisements. Suddenly he thought he had noticed something. He considered for a moment and then turned back a fews pages. A bold heading spread across the adjacent pages of the newspaper:

Union Public Service Commission, National Defence Academy/Naval Academy Examination.

Slowly he walked up to the table, sat down, and started reading the advertisement carefully.

Silence is not peace. A tense quietness pervaded that one-room house-A silence waiting to shear anytime. Ashish and Suchitra were cautious. They had not failed to notice the remoteness in which Vijayant had gradually closeted himself. But they had the typical middle-class patience to live with anxiety so they suffered quietly. But today was different. It was a turning point in the life of the family. Vijayant had succeeded in qualifying for the competition and was selected to join the Army. After years of uncertainty their son had finally found his feet in the world, and that too as per their preference, a government job–assured salary, pension, settled for life. The inherent parental anxiety about the survival of their offspring had been settled. But Ashish and Suchitra were agitated.

"When did you fill out the form?" Ashish questioned angrily.

Vijayant did not reply and kept on packing his bags.

"I am asking something! Who gave you the money for applying... for the exam?" Vijayant suddenly stopped and turned back.

"It wasn't your money."

Ashish was taken aback by the stone-hard expression. Now he wondered how he had missed the change. "You didn't even bother to tell us?"

"You didn't need to know anything?"

"You have joined the Army without even telling your parents! When did you appear for the written? When did you go for the interview?"

"I made it possible... Otherwise, there is always a 'logic'...to find excuses. Nothing great ever came out of thinking logically except an assured mediocrity." Vijayant's voice had a strange gruff as if he was roaring.

"Stop taunting your father. You have qualified today because we gave you that education. Don't forget I am your father and you are my son!"

"And not your property!" Vijayant retorted.

"Where is your sense of responsibility? You are our only son and you have gone and joined the forces. Aren't you supposed to look after us when we grow old?"

"No, I am not! I am not supposed to look after you when you grow old...Look at your sense of entitlement! You are speaking as if I am your slave...your property! As if you own me! So self-centred...selfish! To you, even your child is an investment to secure your future? My purpose in life is to look after you? What was I asking for? To study? And you were not even willing to take that risk! You were not ready to become my guarantor but you feel that I should be the guarantee of your old age. Look at your mindset! All you want is that I should bring in the money and hand it over to you! And now that I have found a way for myself you are feeling offended as if your investment is running away without fulfilling its obligations. That is what we proudly tom-tom as a tradition in this country. As if the whole meaning and purpose of a child's life is to look after his parents, fulfil their failed dreams, and then marry and bring a servant home who can look after them. We have to live throughout as if we owe you something! No, we don't! You haven't made some great sacrifice in bringing me into this world. You looked after me because you were supposed to. You both are responsible for bringing me into this hell that you can't afford. I am the product of your passion and the victim of your sins. Rather each one of us is so. Therefore, that passion remains our fundamental essence. That is what we inherit generation after generation! Whatever! I will not submit to such medieval traditions that perpetually enslave me to selfish interests. This idea, that it is one's duty to look after his parents when they grow old is a ploy, an intoxicant marketed as a tradition by cunning old selfish people like you so that you are looked after once you are disabled and old after having committed all your sins. It is a scheme...To hell with it!"

His mother looked on astounded. She came up to him, held up his face in her palms, and pleaded, "Vicky just look at me...." She wanted to say something, but then she looked into his eyes. She couldn't say a word more and withdrew.

Vijayant walked out of the door without saying anything. His parents looked on hoping he would at least turn once to give them a departing look. But that thought didn't even cross Vijayant's mind.

Chapter Eight

'Wish I could confide in someone. If I were a doctor, I could have understood better.'

Even the hair was starting to grow black. Till now he thought 'it' might be some infection, something temporary, which would run its course and then his same old self will relapse. But 'it' was something more. 'It' had spread further and now covered him almost entirely. Except a few patches that were still 'old', he looked almost forty and felt equally energetic. But he was happy. He was able to move around and do things smoothly. Not a small privilege at all, especially when a few days back he couldn't even bend properly. Being normal is enough. But what about his mind? He examined himself. Unlike his body, his mind didn't feel 'new'. He could remember everything more vividly, and felt the resentments as strongly as if the events had happened just a few days ago. Yet he judged the past from the mature perspective of an old man. And when he did so, he felt that the source of his sadness lay somewhere else and most of his anger was misdirected. To himself and to others, much pain could have been avoided if a few things could have been left unsaid.

Wasn't it true that in the present, man was both his past and future? With his body and his mind, with his memory and his imagination, in this moment he was the condensation of his past as well as his possibilities? He imagined himself standing in the centre of a cyclone with the waves of the past contra- rotating against the waves of the future and the whole then merging into one huge turbulence, rising high, and finally bursting down upon him with its entire weight. Hurled back onto the shores of the present, he scurried out of the bathroom.

'O there was so much stuff in those black boxes! Things after things after things! Things which meant so much at one time.' This marble figurine, he recollected, he had taken leave to go to Agra specially to buy it. Why? Not because he had any idea of its sculptural beauty or symmetry but because it symbolized sophistication in his society. Anyone who possessed it was a man of 'taste'. 'And it was so expensive!' How everyone who visited him was so impressed and he felt so proud. He smiled at how just an object had become his pride, an extension of his ego. But now it had been lying in this box for more than thirty years and everybody including him had forgotten it. How such a small item represented an emotion and a time to which he was tied and held hostage. It was an emotional bondage and he was imprisoned by it. Though, he had packed them away, he wasn't free of them. They still lurked in the deep dark corners. He realized that the origin of his grief ran deep and turning away and letting it lie in the darkness was no solution. If he must be released from his melancholic inertia, he must dig up expose the roots to the light to identify and purge the poison that ran through the fabric of his life.

It was a typical outfit of the seventies. A long collared bright yellow shirt, brown striped bellbottoms and a brown short leather jacket and of course with the accessories including a satin dark brown scarf and a brown leather belt with grooved waves and a copper designer buckle, brown boots and tinted aviator glasses. 'Not bad', he thought looking into the mirror pridefully. Then he started swaggering around the room enjoying the firmness and the smoothness in each step. After a while he came back and sat down on the chair. Releasing his head behind he slowly closed his eyes and breathed in deeply and felt the youth pulsating within him. 'What a gift! what a gift!' his heart whispered to himself. A light jazz music played through his mind and he hummed softly.

The evening rays streaming through the brown curtains filled the room with a golden-orange hue. He opened his eyes and looked around. The soft ambience soothed his soul and filled his heart with a lazy nostalgia. In a languorous sweet mood, he came out and stood in the terrace. The rustle of the leaves to the breeze harmonized with the drift within. The high- and low-rise buildings went up far and beyond standing like musical bars, trying yet unable to culminate. The plane overstrained by the extreme effort of sustaining altitude breathed easy as it descended back to certainty. Somewhere a rail engine blew a long whistle as its wheels screeched and slogged to a halt. Yet on the road mankind and his motor vehicles still hustled with each other, to return to start again tomorrow. The hemisphere sighed out 'relief'.

His wandering eyes floated upto the entrance where the lane opened into the main road. Two women both wearing a saree walked up into the lane. Were these the same two ladies he saw that day? He wasn't sure and he didn't care because his eyes automatically laid upon the slender figure wearing the lemon-coloured saree. She walked unhurried and softly and her slender shoulders, breast and waist flowed with her gentle gait, while a lock fluttered across her eyes. Her fair and supple skin, especially the smooth fold on her waist stood out as the remarkable signature of youth craving a loving touch. Vijayant stood there following her approach unconscious that another young woman was also walking beside her. Simultaneously some instinct whispered that the girl knew that she was being observed and she was enjoying the attention. Suddenly the girl raised her arm to remove the lock from her eyes and simultaneously, looked back at him. Vijayant recoiled from the railings so sharply that his back hit the window behind. He had not been so embarrassed for years.

As he returned to his room he wondered what that look meant. Why did he notice her? Was there someone walking with her? Why didn't he notice the other woman then? Why did he find this particular woman especially attractive? Why does anyone find anyone more attractive than others? There was something more that drew his eyes towards her. She conformed to the pattern embedded deep inside him. He felt a thunder far away in his being and he shuddered.

"Haha! you look so different!", Sumeet chuckled. "These are old-fashioned now! But you look good dad! I'm telling you. I always wondered what you were like when you were young."

"What do you mean? Were you on some other planet when I was young?" Vijayant retorted sharply. But he deliberately avoided looking at his son with a full face.

Sumeet was embarrassed. He said hesitantly. "No, I can't imagine...I mean I can't remember you wearing such clothes. But why are you wearing a monkey cap? It doesn't go along with this."

"I'm not well." Vijayant again tried to avoid him.

"Wow! look at your hands they look so... fresh! I somehow feel that it was good that you went to the hospital. I don't know what they have given you but you look so much better now. Do you remember what they gave you? There is nothing in the prescription! They're only vitamins. Are they helping you? How are you feeling? Let me see. Sumeet walked up to his father."

"Don't touch me I am fine!" Vijayant withdrew sharply. Seeing Sumeet startled, Vijayant explained, "I have just come back from the hospital. I might be carrying some infection so you stay away now."

"Fine fine! You look strange in this dress. But this is good. I think one should live his life fully. But you can still fit in! That's commendable, I can't...fit in my old dresses."

"Where's my Jawa?" Vijayant asked suddenly.

"Huhn?"

"Where's my Jawa, my bike?"

"Oh, that? That we sold long back! I don't and you couldn't... I mean ride a bike...it was just lying there gathering dust you remember?"

"I have to go."

"Go?... where?"

Vijayant stood there contemplating.

"Dad?"

"I have to go on a pilgrimage."

"Pilgrimage!... Why?... Where?"

"You are too old to ask silly questions. Why do people go on pilgrimage? I have to go today rather... now."

Sumeet stood flabbergasted, "Are you serious? Where does this come from suddenly? Listen! I haven't even informed in my office. I won't get leave like that!"

"No! I'll go alone." Vijayant walked up to his Almirah.

"Dad! Dad! OK, OK listen listen! I think there was something in the medicine... it is good you feel better .. stronger, but you have to understand... you are still old. You can't go on a pilgrimage alone. You won't be able to handle it. Plus look at you, we don't know what is happening to you and how this is going to turn out. We need to be careful. You just can't bolt away anywhere. I cannot leave you when you are sick! Give me some time. I will take you on a pilgrimage."

"No Sumeet. You don't need to come along."

"Papa please don't go like this. The shops have just opened up. The infection has not yet gone. If something happens it will be a very big problem for me. How will I find you? How will I manage everything?"

Vijayant kept taking out his clothes from the Almirah.

"Dad if there has been some mistake from our side, if Smita has done something which has offended you then I apologise for ..."

"Sumeet listen!" Vijayant breathed heavily, "You already know how old I am...Both of us know that I do not have many years to live. But still, there are things that I need to resolve before I die. For that, I have to go. I have felt this need for long but I couldn't have gone earlier. But after coming from the hospital, I feel fit enough to go on this...pilgrimage. Rather I feel that this is one last opportunity that has been given to me by time or destiny or whatever there is. So please let me take this chance." Vijayant looked directly at Sumeet with his full face now. Sumeet stood stunned and motionless. "You are a good son Sumeet. You owe me nothing and I don't have any complaints against you...or Smita. I could have gone off without telling you but that would have been a betrayal. I leave you with everything I have. You are not responsible for any consequence and I will give this in writing. I shall also keep you informed about my whereabouts and if I need your help I shall ask you. I will come back if I can't handle it. Just let me go!"

Vijayant walked out with sure steps and a back pack. Sumeet looked on anxiously. Smita was still disoriented. As he walked the first few steps Vijayant was reminded of that evening long back when he had walked out of his parent's house. He knew that if he had to move on, he mustn't look back.

Chapter Nine

It felt strange just to walk out without knowing where to go...just to walk out into uncertainty. He wondered what was wrong with him. He had never gone so...unplanned. Yet there was a strange sense of presence. As he passed by, a sublime scent drew him back. A night jasmine hung over the boundary of a bungalow, its tiny white flowers quivering. When he inhaled deeply, he felt crowned by a divine purity. It was unbelievable! Unconsciously our mind always connects beauty with eyes-It is always something you see. He never realized that even fragrance could raise such sensations that could only be defined as-beautiful. He turned and looked ahead. A glimmering horizon lay before him. It was late evening. Under the sceptre of pandemic, humanity with all his chaos and clamour, had vamoosed beyond the boundaries of visibility. A dewy darkness descended from the sky and filled up the vacancy with moist silence. The spaces and the things filling them shimmered in the lights. Night was the theatre of rich ornamented interplay of the natural and the artificial. A car hushed away somewhere far. As if beauty took a deep breath as she turned in her sleep. Everything was beautiful, meaningful. Where did all this come from suddenly? Where was all this hiding? Or he hadn't noticed it? Forgotten it? For how long! He felt alive.

At a little distance smoke arose from a desolate road side tea stall. He bought a cup of tea and sat down on the bench beside. The first few sips filled him with a warm comfortable leisure. Leisure-he hadn't felt that sensation for so long! He had passed by this stall, the night jasmine so many times in the past, this evening scene had played out in front of his eyes so many times before, he recollected, but he had never considered them. He always had to reach somewhere and they was 'just there', on the way. When he had a purpose the world had no purpose or meaning. But now in this moment of purposeless leisure, suddenly everything seemed so significant, meaningful, beautiful. Then, beauty and meaning was just a waste of time. Now, this was time's very purpose. Perhaps time without purpose is the time actually lived. Perhaps wasting time is the best use of it! He was bemused by his mental wanderings; he was enjoying it as well. Only briefly. Soon his mind swung back to the future. Where was he to spend the night? Afraid 'logic' might convince him to change his mind he had rushed out of the house. Now he needed to put up somewhere. He couldn't go back. He knew there was a three star a kilometre away. To stay in a star hotel barely two kilometres away from home! Preposterous! Audacious!

Vijayant glanced out of the window while he finished his breakfast. 'It must be... what? About eleven?' He was deliberately avoiding looking at the clock yet his obsession with time won't leave him. Frustrated he whispered, "Lived like a clock throughout." He walked up and picked up the newspaper.

Aah! There you are! Advertisements on the first page instead of information!! That's what's most important today hunh? The new product...to be consumed! He folded newspaper and raised it for killing mosquitoes. But there were none. Irritated he flung it at the dustbin. He turned on the television. Again, the modern nuisance-Ads- blared on the home portal. Hurriedly he navigated to the news channels. They in turn were bombarding the peaceful morning with manmade crises in the name of news. 'No point letting the world soil your mind.' Disgusted, he switched off the TV and ambled across the room for a while. Then, after putting an old Indian morning raga on his mobile he went to the bathroom.

Again, he stood in front of the mirror examining himself. Questions and doubts exploded within. 'Why? How? What will come of it, How long does this stay? What now? Will I die?' Yet, despite the turbulence, he was in no hurry. He waited for the water to fill up the bath tub. He had a bathtub in his own bathroom also but he always took the shower because it took too long to fill up the damn cauldron and he couldn't wait. Fast and more is the ethos of the time. It is the measure of efficiency and diligence. But now he was thinking different. Now he was questioning the very pattern of his thoughts and feelings. Gradually, the water filled up the tub and after rechecking its temperature he entered unhurried and laid like a king. The warmth of the water began to rest his thoughts. 'Does it matter? This may be for this moment only, let me just live it,' he thought, scrubbing his body lightly and slowly, softly and carefully as if he was cleaning a fragile artifact entrusted to him by time. Then as the music and the warmth settled him further he closed his eyes. As he dissolved into the silence, he breathed out a faint whisper, 'Feels like I am my soul…that never grows old.'

The liveliness of the moderately crowded market filtered into his being and he felt as if he had returned from a prolonged and monotonous sick leave. He was enjoying his walk along the street. On the surface everything appeared more glamorous, but past, with its piercing bleak eyes, pried through the layers of the present. At some places it lurked round the corners in a very old tailor shop, a provision store or a cycle shop. He could relate to both. He came upon a motorcycle showroom and walking on he cursorily scanned the models on the huge window. Suddenly his eyes fell upon a model that seemed to have been waiting since long. An brand new, old model, olive green Jawa. Classic, they called it.

The thrum of the bike reverberated the youth in his spirit. The air skimmed past his face and he felt on the edge of experience- again. Every turn was a discovery. His well-planned and organized life had always been about reaching somewhere, but now he didn't know where to go. And when you don't know that every stop is a destination. At the traffic signal the road signage indicated the highway at ten kilometers. He thought of getting on it but was deviated by the structure that stood on the other side of the crossing, the huge modern temple of consumerism - The shopping mall.

A man carrying a dog like a baby was arguing with the security to let them in. Passers-by especially women overflowed with oily kindness for the dog .

'Why not? After all dogs also have the right to go around the mall... lift their legs on the things they like or dislike and mark their ownership with their scent. Don't the banks issue credit cards to them? Ooooh! the security is so polite! Looks like they feel guilty for telling him that he can't bring in the dog!

He entered the mall shaking his head in disgust 'Pets-living toys... feel sorry for them. And these pet owners! The worst animal rights violators! Treating an animal like a human is the grossest violation of animal rights. That animal was not born to be like that! It was supposed to live like an animal … … an animal may not have human advantages but that also gives them the 'Freedom' to live by their instincts. True… overtime certain animals and humans have evolved to live together. But that doesn't mean they have become humans! Imagine an animal forced to hold its shit, its piss, till his human father comes back home… and the animals do learn to live in the human environment since they have been there since they were quite young. Isn't that indoctrination… manipulation…tragic?? A being made to forget his own identity!! And if doesn't submit, it is dangerous, deserves no love, no compassion!! We don't love anything or anyone, we just love our perception of it. The moment the other does not conform to that image, an independent dog, wife or even our own child, disenchantment begins and ends up with castigation and hatred. What we call love is the extension of own ego upon the other. Their pets are also the extensions of their owner's ego. And they love them like they love themselves, tenderly. These animal lovers oozing and cooing with love for these 'cute' clean dogs are scared as death of those street dogs, unfortunates suffering and dying of hunger, disease, accidents everyday. How many dog lovers take them as their pets? Just because they are not foreign and good-looking breeds.

Amazing are the advantages of looks. Man has inseminated racism here also.'

He knew he was rambling unnecessarily. But his mind just won't stop. Why was he so resentful? Suddenly he noted that the image of that forsaken shivering dog, the one in the academy, was going around in his mind. 'Compliance! That's what the world wants. I think what animals need is not our love but our indifference, a compassionate indifference- a distance. Be kind and let them be. Because beauty is that point of exact distance from nature from where if you take a step back its invisible and if you take a step closer, its gross. Only if mankind could decipher the exact distance to be maintained from nature, beauty will be. Just maintain that bit of distance, a bit of control on yourself and things will fall in place.'

He felt awkward. People never noticed him so much, but now, especially women, were gazing at him as if he was the last surviving animal of some extinct species. Did he look so out of place in this 70's outfit? And why were these boys staring at him as if he was competing with them? Ah yes! He was. He was competing with them for women. 'Hell no, not again! You can't go all over that again.' As he said this to himself, he suddenly realized that he was placed in a unique situation where he had the eye of the youth but observation of the old. His overall sensory experience, with the vividness of youth and the acuity of old was now more holistic.

He continued wandering and the more he saw the more he perceived and more turbulent he grew. He was convinced that shopping malls were the modern and glamorous version of the old shopping street. 'New ground, old game: New jungle, old hunger.' Boys still hung around ogling at girls passing by, still with their strange haircuts, but now they had a stranger built. Their muscular upper body was incompatible with their thin legs and almost pot bellies. This was further exacerbated by their body-hugging outfits which made them uncomfortable especially around the crotch where they fidgeted regularly. 'Disgusting!' Their heavy eyebrows on a blunt expressionless face conveyed a well-developed mental dullness graduating smoothly towards retardation, self-induced through sustained exposure to absolutely nothing that requires any mental effort. Their raw guffaw exposed a rusticity which only had style and brand to prop up their distorted, half-bred personalities, meant only to impress women and lure them into having sex- animal like. 'How many more generations of men will it take to realize that unlike males, for the feminine gender, as a whole, sex is a 'means' and not the 'end'. It takes only two episodes on any animal channel to figure that out… dumbfucks… Alright! now I understand what that word means. New generation, same illusions. Now look at these two.' Two strangely adorned young women, approached from the other side and then passed by. But the strong odour of the scent they wore lingered on, diverting his perception and thoughts towards women. He was starting to get exasperated.

Most of the girls who were alone did not look around much. 'Just like earlier times' he thought. It was a way of avoiding eye contact with preying males who could misinterpret even a casual glance as an 'invitation' of some kind. But now they remained so immersed in their mobiles that it sent a deliberate message - 'Stay Away!' Yet, all this, while they wore everything that could be construed as an invitation. Their awkward stiff walk clearly indicated their preference for attention over discomfort. The girls in groups seemed a more confident, spoke slightly louder and laughed upon trivialities, all affectations to invite attention. Women managed their contradictory intentions with self lies and subtle manipulations, still.

The small book stall beside the washroom was so secluded, empty and dull it looked like a museum. Most of the books were competition guides 'But why so many self helps? Six way to win…, seven ways to succeed…, Ten ways to achieve…, all providing ready templates to deal with all possible frailties, fears and desires, presenting life as if could be cracked with some formula. I wonder how many authors follow their own prescription and if they do, are they happier? This obsession with perfection creates a perpetual sense of 'deficiency' and continued unhappiness with the present. Though there is no datum to judge nature we can't be sure if it believes in perfection herself. After all, why does it need millions of sperms to fertilise just one egg? Why so many galaxies for one earth? So many seeds for one tree? Perfection seems unnatural, artificial. And that is what this generation is turning out to be – Fake! Can't they live with some deficiencies and forgive oneself some lapses once in a while!' That thought struck him. How easy it was to preach. He felt like one of those hypocrite authors himself.

"How much is this one for please?"

"All those are a hundred each."

"What!"

"Fixed price." The shopkeeper said in a bland tone.

"No that's not the problem!"

The bookseller almost snatched the book from Vijayant's hand and started inspecting it, "Good condition! No problem !"

"No that is not the problem!"

The shopkeeper was perplexed.

"No, these are timeless classics... paragons of literature...why do you sell them so cheap? It's an insult...to the author...to literature, I mean..."

The bookseller looked down smiling. Then he looked at him and indishaking his head side to side spoke politely, "Few people read them sar of few who read...clearing staack now... opening a branded cosmetic store here sar! Not much profit in this ...I have to pay the rent aalso."

"I am travelling... have limited luggage space otherwise I would have bought a few more. Please take two hundred for this book... for the author's sake."

"OK sar... No problem!" The shopkeeper kept smiling, "Sar! You know in Riaz Markit, Classics are sold for hundred rupees Kg!! Knaaledge by weight! Ha HaHa!" He put the book in a gift packet and handing it to Vijayant with both hands said, "Happy to sell you sar, I know you will read it. Many buy but don't read and who read becomes a philasafer... ...just after reading one book Ha HaHa!"

The food court was on the top floor. On the way Vijayant noticed that unlike the book stall the nearby mobile store of a famous expensive brand was well crowded. As he approached the escalator, a group of adolescents passed by.

'Look at these zombies! With friends yet sunk in their mobiles...disconnected with the 'real', living in the 'virtual'. Why? Because it is more agreeable? Comfortable? Instead of dealing with reality they have chosen to escape it. We evolved into the present humans dealing with physical and mental challenges but smart phones, and technology as a whole, is making life so easy that it is enfeebling us. Technology is 'unabling' us by 'enabling' us, making us weak and dumb. Worst, it is concentrating data and knowledge in a few hands. Earlier we talked about concentration of political power, regimes and dictators and so on, but today it is about concentration of data with a few individuals or organizations. And such entities will be supra national that will make governments and borders redundant. Huf!... ... Humans are 'social' animals? Ha! Humans are herd animals! Cows and lambs! How naively we just follow the trend, go along and just surrender our destiny to others! And all herds have a shepherd. A 'Good' Shepherd! ... ...Smart phones, dumb people! And few who aren't dumb are either masters or pariahs. Age of reason, Age of information, Age of dullness and then extinction, this is how it'll all end!'

He stepped off the escalator, walked a few yards looking around then halted. Though moderately crowded because of the pandemic yet this was the most crowded floor in the mall. Food outlets lined the boundary of the floor, one after the other, offering unlimited quantity and variety of food. Yet people were anxious as if food was running out. The fattest ones were even more nervous, probing the stalls like cows looking for their feed tubs and the stalls offering the most bright and glittering calories had queues.

'Probably it was Plato who said 'Necessity is the mother of invention', but marketing is the mother of necessity. That is what marketing does. That's what the free-market economy is all about, creating the need, the demand - from frailties, fears and dreams of the people. When the laser was invented, they said it was an invention that was looking for a job. And then they found its applications, many indeed. Look at that queue at that Pizza outlet. Did people need pizza and then it was invented? No it was innovated, repackaged and then marketed and that is how its need was created. Its smooth flowing liquid cheese, was injected into the minds of the people as a necessity for birthdays, parties, family friends, pleasure, happiness and then... people started demanding it, and those marketeers made millions and became 'Business Leaders!'. They don't want humans any more, they want consumers ...because humans are rational but consumers are animals...who 'dare' to 'live' their passions.' That's what the billboard in front said. 'In the industrial economy you manufacture 'things' but in a market economy you manufacture 'demand'. And food? Look at these nervous obese bastards! Its unbelievable they think they even need to eat! Look at that anxious fat fellow, worried, probably because his token hasn't been called out yet...because he is afraid of the discomfort of hunger. While the poor die of starvation in the remote parts of this country this man is scared of his own hunger! And they have fed him so much for so long he believes that that much is necessary. And they feed him more and more because he can buy it, even if he doesn't need it, he demands it. Food industry! They don't grow food any more, now they manufacture it. And we have become like domestic animals on a farm who are fed and fed and fed and then their money is milked and milked and milked out of them! This is what they call development?

Everything is a scam!...Don't fell like eating anymore...Let me get a drink... ...It has been a while.'

He looked at the signage curiously. 'Is there a dance club out here? There were not many when I was young. Well I am young now! He smiled and then looked at his watch.'

An extremely bright bar stood in the centre of a dark mephitic hall, intervened by flickering lights and wandering lasers. A strange cloudy smell filled the darkness. Vijayant walked straight up to the bar. He had never been to a civilian night club before. He was used to the Officers' Mess which was much simpler and very much cheaper. He wondered what will it cost for all this glamour and glitter. Even though there was no point in saving money now, yet it seemed criminal to spend too much money on losing one senses. Hesitating a bit, he asked for the menu. The bartender looked at him awkwardly and then started looking for it.

'All liquor taste the same only some are slow and some are fast acting. Its actually the hangover that decides their quality. What! Five hundred for a drink!' He went over the menu with such big eyes that others around started noticing. As it is his outfit and conduct made him look like a time traveller. He wanted to avoid drawing further attention. 'Beer would be safe', he thought.

There was moderate crowd on the dance floor. Most of the people were bystanders, there to get a drink shaken or stirred with glamour, with a tinge of sensuality. That is expensive. Few couples and mostly groups of men and women were dancing among themselves. All of them, when they came to the dance floor, were graceful and smooth but as the drinks went down, their movements became more and more vigourous until their smooth conscious movements transmogrified into a fit of rustic, uncontrolled, disconnected, all hell break loose madness which would make even a gorilla beating his chest look civilised. It was strange to see others appreciate such madness as some kind of boldness. 'We had less money but more class.' A man sweating profusely came down the dance floor and passed by to get a drink. 'It's a strange pungency when the sweat mixes with deodorant. Thank you for wearing the deo anyways!' Vijayant muttered to himself.

The beer tasted awful. Suddenly he realized that the offensive smell all around was the cocktail of all the liquor in the bar and going around. Others were enjoying their drinks.

'Am I finally over it?'

Weekends had become synonymous with drinking while he was in service. Friday evenings were for letting his hair down. He would take a drink and then another and then time would just fly by. The fact was that liquor altered his understanding of time and reality. The evenings that he got drunk remained as clouded and dizzy memories. Certain evenings he was so drunk that the only memory were the Saturdays and Sundays, spent on just recovering from its terrible hangover. And yet, it never occurred to him he was an alcoholic! Why? Just because he didn't drink everyday? But now he knew that if you imagine filling even a second of your time with 'just one', you are an alcoholic. A non-alcoholic mind never imagines alcohol.

'How dissipation is promoted as disport¿ How poison is sold as pleasure¿ How bitter is the flavor of 'class'¿ How odour is a class of aroma¿ How stupefaction is relaxation¿ How distortion is definition¿ How manipulation is marketing¿ How decadence is modernity¿ How madness is freedom¿ How many more generations will it take to realize, they don't just seek to sell us but they want to enslave us, by addicting us. They don't sell us, we sell us, our time, our body, our mind, our reality, our existence! Good riddance! No, can't be sure! Never! Never let down guard against this maleficent spirit!'

'But why do we drink at all? Drinking boosts dopamine in the brain!! But why does it boost dopamine in the brain?? Why doesn't, say, mathematics boost dopamine in the brain?? Because alcohol makes you less conscious, loosens control, releases you from the burden of civilisation - this fakedom of civility that we wear upon the animal that we actually are. Yes! right! This reason, rationality, formality, control, civilization: It is constraining, suffocating, stressful... and then comes alcohol!...unshackling us from this 'Kingdom of Fakedom' and allowing us to live our delusions which is zillion times better than reality : And when that happens, then the brain releases dopamine and we feel happy. Freedom, therefore, is not some great aspiration for the day of deliverance from some tyranny but the agitation of the animal within clamouring to be unleashed!!!! See! I got drunk, cursing alcohol. Again it won. I told you!' He shook his head, kept the glass on the bar and got ready to leave.

"You don't look like you belong here."

"No I don't... sort of."

Though he looked young yet Vijayant had enough years behind him to know the real intent of her question. Many other men stood at the bar, but she had chosen him. At his age he was aware of the peculiar attraction of women towards the 'different'. A projection of their own ego to stand out. Women are primarily indirect players. Instead of doing they get things done for themselves. They fulfil their wishes through others-mostly men. She had taken a chance, yet her voice betrayed the nervousness behind her confidence. But he wasn't interested. Why? He was curious himself. He looked at her and both their eyes met momentarily. 'Damn! If she had met me forty years before!' He could sense the competing vibes of men around him. Yet, within him that 'pull' was missing. He had never felt so free.

"You're here with friends?"

"Yeah... sort of." She said drawing out the word smoothly.

'Yeeeah!, this ultimate expression of fake casual modernity. 'Yeeeah they say it with such a drag. Why can't they just say 'yes'.' But a pub was no place to correct a youngster.'

"I am with my colleagues. They are there..." She indicated towards the dance floor.

"You are not dancing?" He couldn't find anything other than the banal question. Out of practice! He thought.

She shook her head, "Too much crowd."

'What were you expecting, on a dance floor?' He didn't say that. There was no point in acting a quick-wit. There was no need to impress anyone.

A pregnant silence. He could feel her wait...expecting him to continue the conversation. He looked at her askance once again surveying her from head to toe. She was wearing a simple makeup, jeans and tee shirt, nothing ostentatious. Not trying to be too coy either. There was an authenticity about her.

'This youngster is a neophyte on exploration. Might be some employee in a corporate, a novice on adventure. But she doesn't look like one of those facile, deceitful smooth talkers.'

'It's not easy to hold a conversation. 'Hold': to maintain the interest in the conversation and use it as an instrument of own 'will' over others. It's a subtle art. Few are able to do that. Most of us are barely able to communicate. Very less of what we

114

feel can be put into words, rarely into the right words and even lesser is understood by the listener. Despite our words, language, speech, we are barely able to communicate accurately.'

"So you're with friends yet alone." He said.

"Wow! do I look ... lonely?" She said smiling.

"Do I look lonely?"

She nodded slightly, smiling.

"Colleagues are not friends." He said

She raised her brows to show she was impressed, "You have experience!"

"And wisdom."

"What do you do?" She asked.

"Nothing at all!"

She was confused by his confidence. No man would say that.

" I don't need to."

She raised her eyebrows.

"I have earned whatever I had to. We earn more than we need... Drink?"

"No, I don't drink. I'll buy a soft drink for myself. Why aren't you dancing?"

"Because I am single."

"Rich and single that's odd !"

"That's the best."

She was more interested now, but he felt weary and stale in his mouth.

'Go over all this, all over again? Outcome? Wounds, enduring wounds. Extreme pleasure the cause of extreme sadness. Can't lose this solitary paradise.' As he curled into himself he noticed more women around him giving him 'looks'.

'Angels of grief.' What would be an achievement in the past seemed an entanglement now.

'Attraction, attachment, love, sex, relationship, revulsion –milestones to misery. Youth-The launch pad to greatness, misemployed for diving into degeneration. A divine light lost in the darkness of desires. Wish I could caution them. But who would listen? I said, new generation-same mistakes.' He began to leave.

"Are you leaving?"

"This isn't for me. Let me see something else."

"Oh! you mind If I come along?"

'Huh! women and the world! Images and illusion. Try to hold on to them, they vanish, Try to get away, you find them dangling over your shoulders, like a dead body... now carry them around!'

A number of couples hung around in the lobby outside the club, occupying the stairs chairs, sills and every possible place.

'Ah! Lovers!! pioneers of modernity. Free Sex!- the fashion of freedom! Why do they have to fall all over each other in public? Is it love or its proclamation? Do they think they are doing something nobody has done before? If you are so overflowing with it why can't you get a room for yourselves? Everything is just for display. Earlier such display was blasphemous. But what was blasphemy once is belief today, what was egregious then is fashion today. We were more discreet but we were intense. Look at this guy, walking with a girl, dawdling like he forgot to wipe his arse! Government should arrest ugly and dirty men dating a beauty like that for causing trauma to other more deserving men! One can be sure like the Newton's Law that public display of affection is directly proportional to the speed of disenchantment. This is not love, this is not even sex, this is just fashion.' As he walked away he realised that 'drawing attention' was the zeitgeist of the times and the youth of today sought to achieve it by taking two opposite routes. One-standing out, Two-Following the crowd. 'They are all bunch of half cocks!'

As he came up the escalator and stood in the central lobby his thoughts over the last few hours started distilling.

'This shopping mall is a sample of the society that we are evolving into. Glittering dead. There was always an artificiality, superficiality, impermanence, hollowness, weakness, instability, unreliability around but now, it has absorbed into the spirit and become a part of it. As if reality has lost its soul...and everything and everyone has become mechanical, not only doing but even thinking, behaving, smiling, talking without feeling. There is nothing left in us...to hold on to.'

Why did he feel like that? Was something was wrong with him? Why all the glamour around failed to gratify him. Why was he so weary? He just wanted to get away. But this girl following him! So beautiful and original, she made him so resentful that he pitied her. Perhaps it was the society and the people and the disgust he felt for them or perhaps there was something wrong within. Ever since he could remember he felt this persistent sadness within himself, as if he was not able to feel things fully. Everything seemed worthless, meaningless, like the sour aftertaste left on the tongue after a viral, only that it was permanent, making the whole life taste sour. That is what he wanted to strip away so that he could feel life fully like an innocent. A permanent gloom hung over his existence. Suddenly it occurred that he had left his house. For what? And he walked out of the mall briskly, alone.

Chapter Ten

'Palimpsest! Like a palimpsest!'

Cruising through the broad avenue lined by boundary walls on both sides, the murals, graffiti, political slogans and advertisements passed like a series of varied images in a musical bioscope. As he swerved closer he could see the traces of what was scribed on them before it was overwritten, or even before the previous layer. The past staring at the present or, the past staring at the past... in his case. 'These walls- Palimpsests, overwritten again and again yet the grooves and traces of the past remain. Aren't we all overwritings over the past? Eyes of my father looking through me! Then what would be the palimpsest? This moment? Me? Me in this moment? Or 'me' is a moment? I am the moment and the memories. And each moment contains traces of the past and the past of that past back upto the beginning? Yes traces of our past right upto our animal ancestors lurk within us. Not only the physical aspects but also the mental. We don't need to go to the Galapagos Islands like Darwin. Our origins are right here within us, the origin of our species as well as the origin of our grief. The darkest and the deepest endures.'

'From the flyover, he could see the traffic jamming up ahead. Swarms of vehicles lined up, along and behind each other, like a huge flock lost in the middle of a track. Following vehicles rushed and then crammed up into the traffic ahead.

A driver overtook him, blaring his horn, and giving him a stare. He stared back and murmured, 'What are you rushing towards? Death? All your agitation is pointless, your purpose...meaningless! your time, your money ... worthless!' As he crawled to a stop and looked around he felt a barrenness within, like an abandoned boat in a hopeless sea. His anger condensed into poetic disgust.

Me, We, Society,
In a stupor,
Back and for(th),
Afraid to stop
And take stock,
In the inertia of motion,
In a stupor-of delusions.

A political procession had jammed the road. The police had arrived and had managed to move them to a side and the traffic slowly opened up. As he passed, he saw a politician standing in an open truck with his aides and assistants. A large number of his supporters followed in muscular SUVs raising victory slogans. Crowds gathered around to catch a glimpse of the 'leader' whose face was buried under the contoured mountain of garlands. While most people were idlers, some of them, with their eyes filled with adoration, seemed loyal followers.

'Who was that young army captain... in Africa, who overthrew the elected government? ...and the people were so happy! Then the dictator went about in an open truck like this...surrounded by commandos, wearing new fatigues and ferocious looks and people! They rejoiced! Cheered! Shook his hand! And the news anchor was all praise for his youth, his looks! his virility!...sure, why not!! That's what you need to run the country, virility!!!... not maturity but virility... with gallons of sperms! Even some neighbouring countries supported the coup and were ready to attack 'imperialists' trying to interfere! This is a government of a country or some Band of Brothers movie? OK! The elected government was corrupt. But what about the military junta? Are they all so corrupt less?'

'But the point is-what makes people believe that someone else will come and resolve their problems. Why do they believe that one day someone would descend from the skies and sweep away all their problems by some miraculous sway of his magical sceptre and all their wishes will come true and then they will live happily ever after in some la la land!!!! Wherefrom comes this idea of the...the messiah...the day? We have woven fiction around men and made them prophets and Gods, heroes and leaders. We want someone to protect us, to submit to and to be led by, an alpha male or a mother cow. Freedom is scary. We want someone to surrender to, who can then take over us and our responsibilities and solve our overwhelming life for us. And reality?.... reality follows the natural laws and processes and is therefore hopeless, unbearable and so they have manufactured miracles and from those miracles, hope. There is no God! No one to help you! Face it! Only then you can solve your problems.'

The traffic opened up and all the vehicles broke loose. The anxiety to rush out was so infectious that even Vijayant sped up abruptly, till he realized he had nowhere to go. Vehicles around him blared and overtook him viciously.

'Hurry! Hurry! Hurry! Slaves! They're afraid if they are late they will be humiliated. Humiliation hurts. More painful than pain is the anticipation of pain. That's what these people are afraid of and therefore they are rushing towards! No, they are not rushing towards but running away. The traffic dispersed and he cruised along the turn his bike slanting a bit.

'We? We were rebels! I tell you! we were disliked but we were bloody independent! Resistance was heroism, compliance was sycophancy, deviance was leadership and failure!...Failure was martyrdom! But today! Truth is blasphemy, forthrightness is rebellion, lies are comfortable and submission is decency... Know what freedom feels like?? When you don't need...no...don't expect anything!! From anyone!! Not from yourself! Not even from God! True freedom is to be free even from god! Even if he exists!!' The bike ride filled him with a sense of defiant manliness.

Long after I had wished,
My wish was fulfilled,
By that time my soul had dried,
And my heart, my mind had killed.

God thought he had returned my prayers,
But I stopped wanting long back,
I'm a new man on a one way road,
And I don't intend to turn back.

Now it seems God is worried,
He's no longer in my thoughts,
I can tell you, to be completely free,
Man must be first free of God.

God and hope get us addicted,
To the status quo of misery,
Letting go requires great courage,
And walking away is a great victory

I'm not the one who picks up crumbs,
With a bent back and thankful eyes,
I am the owner of my hell,
I am the king of my paradise.

'But this is not the age of freedom, this is the age of success. Success brings honour, power, wealth and stress... Success is stress misspelt.' He smiled at the thought. He noted the signage above. 'Problem is that the pace has changed. Machines reduced the effort and time to do the work but then we increased the quantity : Because we wanted more done... ...so back to square one. Now we are overwhelmed. The more we have the more we need but what we actually need is time... ... ...to do nothing. But we have become machines, doing doingdoing without stopping ... living without thinking.'

Impelled by greed,
Mounted the expanding cycle of needs,
Lost in running, speed,
Now we can't breathe,
But now- we can't leave.

There was little traffic here. He had reached the suburbs. 'From disorganized organization to organized disorganization.' He gazed at the villager sauntering down the street. 'No job, No hurry, no money, no options, just the present. Doesn't seem to be missing anything. Ignorance is bliss. Someone said they can easily go without food for a day or two and me! I think I will die if I don't have breakfast.' A country lass carrying a bag passed by, 'Wow saw that face! Look at those arms! Can break the neck of a city chic with a click, that's hard work and pure diet!'

'Even the sun is relaxing here, trees look so serene.' A line of lush green trees hung over both sides of the road for some distance. Light filtered through the breezy leaves sparkling occasionally, filling the waning afternoon with a warm laziness. He eased up on the accelerator and absorbed the scene. 'Pleasure is not happiness; Comfort is not ease.' He shook his head. 'But peace is better than even happiness. Happiness is the high point on the graph...followed by the low point, but peace! It's the absence of the graph! Nothingness! Equanimity! Cities are madlands...should have been a philosopher... ... may be a poet.'

Now the trees were marked with a white band around the trunk and appeared pruned. As he moved further, the road finally opened up into the military area. Training grounds with obstacle courses, field training stands and basketball courts were laid out on both sides of the road. The cleanliness, uniformity and the organization filled him with a pleasant nostalgia. He slowed down. 'Wait! did I take a turn right at the signal? I thought I had gone straight. Cchh! When you know a road it always looks straight. Have not been here for what? About twenty years? Still landed up here! Habit! You get into the habit of doing things and then you do it like a automaton. When we repeat a job the same way again and again the mind learns to do it the same way. Neuropathways are built in the brain and it make less effort in repeating a particular pattern. Gives it space to do more important things. No simple matter. Life is collection of habits! Even the way you think!... that's also habit. What about your own thinking habits VJ?'

He passed by, slowed down, stopped, looked back, turned and came back. A Centurion tank, a war trophy, stood on a platform at the main entrance of the training ground. He dismounted his bike and walked up. Forgotten, worn out, proud, it stood simmering in the setting sun as if the battles of afternoon still raged within. In that unmoving silence his breath blew like a drift and turned the pages of his memory.

"You don't have a four-wheeler!" She looked what the girls from well to do families look like. Fully loaded. Fair, smooth, sharp, beautified, a shoulder less top and navy-blue jeans, all tight fit to exaggerate all the curves that are the privileges of youth. She could easily have been a model but was happy being the alpha female of this bunch of pretentious college students. Reinforced by a hollow pride and well supported by shallow minds she stood, ahead of her group smirking.

"No." Vijayant replied blandly.

"What do you drive then?"

He thought for a moment then said, "Sixteen-wheeler."

"Sixteen-wheeler! Are you a truck driver?" The other members of the group laughed.

"You can call it a truck also... but its more than that?"

"Like?"

"You won't understand."

She looked offended, "Stop playing puzzles. Is your father a transporter or what?"

"No."

"Oh is he the truck driver then?" Sunny, one from the group said mocking.

Vijayant surveyed the faces in the group, each face wearing a scorn looking at him in disgust as if he was a street dog.

"I can show you if you want. But you will have to come to the place where I can show you."

"Why can't you bring that vehicle here?"

"It's a truck I can't bring it in the college."

"Ok where ?" She said impatiently.

"Its a little of the main axis but I'll tell you the way."

"Leave it Sonali, you don't know what he is." Sunny whispered.

"When?" Sonali responded as if she was accepting some challenge.

"Six O' clock, in the morning."

"Well! I don't wake up at night."

"Then you tell the time?"

"Well we will come early in the morning, say around... eleven?"

"It will be late afternoon for me but if you insist..."

"K tell me the way and I'll see you there."

The group was walking back to the class room. Sunny was worked up.

"Its a military area, empty, barren, why has he called us there? These people can be dangerous."

"Why are you guys so scared? He has come for a cadre in our college we'll just go and see... we are so many of us!"

"Do weeee also have to be there?????"

Of course! How could you even think otherwise!"

Everyone looked at each other. "Why do she even want to know what he is, just let him go." Sunny mumbled.

"We should have come at six!!" Sunny said squinting his eyes in the dazzling sun.

The group, stood on a raised feature in the middle of a dusty barren. Scattered with dry thorny bushes, the ground dipped immediately and then rose up undulating right upto a bleak horizon. Used to congestion of the city life, they stood facing all sides wondering if they had landed on an alien planet. The sweltering sun scorched the earth and scalded Sonali's soft skin. She tried to save it by wearing a cap and big goggles. She looked at Sunny doubtfully.

"Yeah, I asked him again yesterday." Sunny pleaded, "Its here only...Look Look! that dust column!!

"Do you feel the wind? It's so hot! you know this is the loo! They taught in geography remember!" A girl in the group said.

"Oh shit! This is so cool! I mean hot!" Another youngster was equally amazed.

"I'm getting sun burns, I got a facial just yesterday, I'll turn dark," said the darkest girl in the group. "Sonali! Can we go back?"

Sonali stared at her, "It' s not eleven yet."

"Is there something there behind that hillock!" Sunny pointed.

A dust column could be seen approaching behind the raised ground. "Its..Its coming closer, Is it him?"

As the dust column came closer, the barrenness shivered with the cacophony of clanking metals, the trembling earth shook away the lose sand which rose up giving the impression as if the earth was vaporizing. From the dead ground immediately beneath arose a metal monster howling, with its gun raised towards the sky like a huge victory sword and slammed bang right in front of them. Bathed in dust the group stood paralysed."

Sunny, first to come to senses cried, "By god! it's a tank, it's a battle tank!"

After grumbling for a while, the tank shut down, and the stillness regained it expanse. Suddenly the cupola opened with a clank. The group was startled. Vijayant emerged from inside and stood on top of the turret in his black military overalls with epaulettes of lieutenant on his shoulders. Now it was his turn to be pretentious.

"I told you it's a sixteen-wheeler, he claimed. See! eight wheels on both sides. You can count them if you want."

Sunny mocked, "Wow that was filmy! Wonder whom that was meant for."

Faced with the truth Vijayant blinked... and then looked at Sonali.

After a long time Vijayant felt a freshness in his heart and a brightness in his mood. More than that something within him perceived that with the change in his temperament the world around him also changed. When he casually thanked the waiter for tea, the entire mess staff organized a party for themselves. Even the teetotallers got drunk. When he acknowledged the salute with polite smile, instead of a return salute, he noted the sentry blush like a child. For the first time Vijayant didn't care about his work and he found that it worked. Somehow or the other the work was completed, whether he was there or not. In his absence his rifle company prepared without his supervision and even won the basketball competition. He was not as indispensable as he thought. 'Thank God!'. Rather there was a thankfulness in everyone's eyes as if they thirsted for nothing more, just a drop of kindness and even wars could be managed. People respect competence but they love humaneness and love is more powerful than respect.

Every day with Sonali was eventful. Every day they would find some new place and wander around till late in the night. Some days they would find an isolated corner in a restaurant and spend hours talking meaningless inconsequential nonsense. Vijayant spoke nonsense for the first time after childhood and he found it quite interesting. For the first time he noted men noticing him. In the world of men, company of women is a mark of superiority over others, but having a girl like Sonali beside him was as good as coronation. Every day she told him something special about himself. For Vijayant it was nothing less than self-discovery. Women know how to make someone feel really special. He liked it when she waited upon him and when she was concerned about what he was eating or drinking. After a long time he felt he meant something to someone. When he returned to his room the memory of her scent entered along, when he closed his eyes her face hung over him. Longing for the warmth of her body and her breath, he lay sleepless, until his restlessness wore him out.

But like every pleasure this pleasure also gradually began to plateau and then fade. Words, sentences, stories, responses became repetitive and predictable. Lately, Sonali seemed more and more overbearing and intrusive and even though he spent so much time with her, she could barely grasp his feelings. She lacked empathy and understanding and their communication remained incomplete. Rather she always brought everything down to status and money. But what was most annoying was that though so beautiful and glamorous herself she barely had any comprehension of beauty and symmetry. Under her softness lay a barren heart. The smooth weather passing, Vijayant slowly retreated into his grey sullen isolation. He felt caught up, hemmed in like a plant in an enclosure, unable to break free and become a tree.

"Jai Hind Sir! There is a call for you", the mess waiter whispered in his ears.

It was expected. Vijayant excused himself from the group and walked inside the telephone room.

"Hello!"

"Hi! Where are you?"

"How are you?," He emphasized as if to say 'You should have asked that first.' But he didn't say it.

There was a murmur on the other side, "I am fine? You?"

"I am also fine." 'She didn't get what I meant, that's what I'm talking about!'

"Where are you missing?"

'You are missing... the point.' "Oh I was a little busy!"

"But I am missing you."

"FFoo!" Vijayant breathed out on the mouthpiece involuntarily.

"Ah! you're bored?

"No Sonali, I am tired."

"Come to me then, I will make it fine"

"There is an official gathering in the mess today."

"When will that nonsense get over?"

"I don't know...Ten thirty or so."

"Can't you come after that?"

"At night? I told you I am tired."

"Please for once!"

"So late! for what?"

"You won't regret it I promise."

"Sonali can't it be some other time! We have PT in the morning, I'm engaged early in the morning."

"Can't you do even this for me? Can't you come to meet me even for five minutes??"

"I am not a college student like you!"

"VJ...no one is at home tonight!!!"

Both went quiet. In the silence both could hear the deep breaths on the other side and felt its moist warmth on their own upper lips.

Vijayant parked his bike close by another house. Basic common sense. Then he took a walk round the colony park and having done the reconnaissance sneaked into the block she'd told him. 'Clever Thieftain!' The door was ajar. Darkness stared through the opening like a scared child. He looked back to make sure no one was watching. A misty dark desolation looked back at him. He entered and came on the threshold a dimly lit foyer. On the other side, under a dull yellow night, stood Sonali . She wore something very thin, like chiffon, through which her curves and her dark undergarments could be made out. She stood with her legs slightly crossed, with inside of her thighs softly overlapping each other. Vijayant crossed the foyer.

Her firm breast held softly inside the cups of her bra, her slender chest rose and fell like an anxious wave. Coming from outside he could feel the quivering warmth rising from her body. Her open hair fell smoothly on her silken shoulder from where a strange scent arose pulling him towards her neck. He put his hand around her waist softly and bent upon her face. Porcelain was her skin! Her lips–Rose!

It was strange. She looked back-pleading. Rather than lust, her eyes held the expressions of a nervous child, on the edge. This woman, so domineering! the alpha female of her group was now surrendering herself to him like a lamb to butcher! She had just given herself up to him as if she had no will, no power, no control! Just total surrender! Even though it was she who called him here. She wasn't ready to own her own desire! She wanted to play victim and leave all responsibility upon him?? A revulsion rose from his spleen, travelled up his throat and Vijayant repelled apart. Astonished, she looked at him. Without saying a word he left. Forever.

He rolled his finger over the metal. It was cold, rough, with a thick layer of dust, paint peeling at places exposing the rust within. The mud guards, the side skirt plates, the bogey wheels still holding fort and the gun watching the darkness. Took a deep breath in, of pride, immediately followed by a prolonged breath out, of dull embarrassment. 'Was no need for all that. Not meant for vain display, least to impress a girl, but to fight, for country, for duty, for honour, Stupid!' Disappointed with himself he shook his head and went back to on his motorcycle, lighting a cigarette on the way.

'But she was a good! Damn! she was so smooth and... fresh. Not like these dry fruits these days. Could have blamed me, but never got back again. That's character! Or probably she felt the same as me! Wonder where she is these days? Alive? Must be seventy-five, eighty or what? These days if you do this! she will follow you to your grave, then lodge a police case, molestation, court? And you will be dug out from your grave and punished, even if you didn't touch the pudding. And then the society? Humiliation! Laws! Courts! Are men only to blame? How people lumber around in the courts for decades! Women still being raped in villages, while men are embroiled in false cases of dowry, molestation. No matter the laws, vulnerable continue to suffer. Some Rajesh, was it? No Rakesh, in the colony, blamed by the girl, took twenty-five lakhs (*$50,000*) to take back the case. Didn't get married. Who would marry after this? When you equate masculinity with animality, men start behaving like women. When you make femininity humiliating then women start behaving like men. That's what is happening today. All evolving into queers. I tell you in the end everyone will become a bunch of quarrelling queers and then we will all die and become extinct. Good! that would be the end of all nonsense! Then peace! When we have a society where both manliness and womanliness are analogous to anomalous then being queer is the only option left! Who says laws and beliefs do not affect human behaviour? If elephants can stop growing teeth because they are being hunted for it why can't men and women have altered sexual orientation when any behaviour attributed to their gender is seen as regressive? We adapt to our environment and laws and beliefs pervade the environment like air. But what's worst is that in all this conflict between man and woman both have lost their essence-love. Ah! Hypocrite'

'It's so quiet here!' It was already dark by now. The tank stood in the dull orange light. The silence was interrupted by the intermittent chirpings of the crickets, and occasional passing of vehicles. 'So different from the city, clean, fresh, heaven! Ah! see the full sky! Its blue, dark blue, the stars like particles. What do they call the smallest particle? Spark or is it quark or they have found something even smaller! They keep on finding something smaller and smaller. When will they realize matter is nothing but...but energy...flowing in this dark space-time like water in the course of a stream, interacting and overlapping with each other and bonding and becoming particle, then protons, electrons, so on, then atoms, bonding with each other and organizing into molecules then organizing, cells, organizing into organs, organisms! That's why they are called organisms because they are organized! Energy is organized! Matter is organised energy! What we call nothing is nothing but energy, like this sky. Earth : Just a drop in this infinite river called universe. Me? :Also a smaller drop, jumping out of water and looking into it. And life? What is life?'

'Like the sapidity of water. Matter and spirit are not dualities but two aspects of the same thing. Every matter has a corresponding character. Simple matter, simple character, complex matter, complex character. So, from the stone to the earth everything has character, that's what we call spirit. This tree, this also has a spirit, only the nature of the spirit is different. So does the universe, its spirit, the combined spirit of everything living and dead in it. The universe lives. There is nothing dead.' He threw the cigarette.

'Huh!' He sniggered. 'Me and my thoughts! Always rambling wandering away somewhere, unable to reach anywhere. Life didn't go as planned. Maybe it was my destiny. Destiny? is there anything like destiny? Nothing. Destiny is the difference between what we think should happen and what actually happens. Things happen just as they were supposed to happen. It is only that we feel that it should have happened some other way. Destiny Ha! ... extension of our ego, again. 'I'. 'I'. Keeps us in the centre of everything, so we believe that whatever is happening is happening for me. It isn't! Everything from birth to death, from the formation of an atom to a human being is just chance.

But we? We are too egoistic to acknowledge that. It must have some meaning! No Brother! It is you who's trying to insert a meaning into it, according to your own understanding. Why? Because that's the nature of 'I'. Mind is the 'character' of the body, its spirit, its sapidity, and 'I' is the centre of the mind, the sun of the spirit, holding this Mind-Body complex together. Keeping itself at the centre this 'I' imposes a meaning on the universe to find a meaning for itself. Survival Instinct of a complex being. Every man is the centre of his own universe. But the truth is-this universe... existence... it exists for its own sake. It has its own universal spirit, the combined spirit of everything living and dead in it. And if you can dissociate with this 'I' and align with that universal spirit, then! ...

What's the time? Eight! Will have to check in somewhere.' He started his bike and got on the

138

road. Tearing that dark emptiness the bike raced louder, brighter, faster...

Chapter Eleven

Lucknow 175 Kms, the highway signage indicated with the broad straight arrow. 'Half this road was the highway, when I came...about sixty sixty-two years back. It was narrow. Was greener then. How many lanes are there? One two three OK six! Broad! There's no gap between the cities now. Its one continuous stretch of habitation all the way. Nature has receded. Every stretch, every piece has been seized, snatched, taken away, from every other being. As if no body else has the right...'

'Why are you going there? There was nothing left, everything was wiped out...burnt away. Remnants?'

"Mumma! When will the light come!" Vijayant sat on the bed facing the table along side in the corner of the room. A lighted candle stood on the table under which lay copies and textbooks, open and closed, playing hide and seek in the flickering light. Sweating in the sweltering darkness, insects and mosquitoes hovered around him, biting his rashes and the prickly heat, puncturing his legs under the table. Vicky grimaced in discomfort.

"It will come." Mother cried out from the kitchen. The faint light of the candle inside the kitchen quivered on the floor outside.

"Its gone for so long!" Vijayant scowled as he wiped the sweat off his face.

"Ok!" Suchitra emerged from the kitchen into the dim light and came to him. She wiped his face with the end of her saree and said, "Let's read Hanuman Chalisa (*Verses in praise of Hindu monkey God Hanuman–One who delivers from crisis*), then you'll see."

"No! it doesn't work! I can't study, can't sleep also! Mumma, can I skip school tomorrow?"

"Papa will be angry..." She took a deep breath, "Study Vicky study! that's your only way out of this hell. Next year class twelfth! board exams!" She bent and held his face in her palms. Both looked at each other. In the dull orange light, sweat sparkled on their faces. "All we can give you is a good school Vicky." Then wiping her own face she went back to her kitchen.

Vicky tried hard for a while but couldn't concentrate. Deviated, he picked up the note book under the light. Sketches of goddess Durga's face were drawn page after page, experimented with, from different angles, with different expressions, but with the same features, that of the the goddess' face that hung over the bed. He sharpened his pencil. Then he turned and looked at the Durga's face. Only half her face could be seen in the candle light. For a moment he thought something. A strange calmness settled on his face.

"Set your bag as per the time-table and get to the bed right now!" Mother stood under the fan wiping the sweat of her face. Electricity had been restored.

"I don't want to sleep right now!" It was an irritated retort. The electric supply had interrupted his flow.

"No! you never know when the light goes again! Catch some sleep before its out again and we spend the whole night awake soaked in sweat."

The daily routine completed like a machine, the household went to bed, set on living the next day the same way. But in that dim mercury nightlight, Vicky lay awake weaving his hopes and thoughts into dreams, that divine face in the background, till the real and the unreal dissolved into one, blurred and then dissolved into oblivion.

Sweating in his winter uniform, he pedalled his old clanking bicycle hard. As he rushed through the fog and approached the school, he could hear the school bell ringing. He pedalled harder. An old and rough Gurkha, probably an ex-soldier, manned the school gate. Age had not abated his soldierly obsession for time. No matter rain, fog earthquake or apocalypse, he would stand in his old khakis, bent, holding one gate with his arm as if manning some border crossing, surveying each child keenly to screen out the terrorist amongst them. The perpetual sneer on his face conveyed his fondness for children as well as their parents and he was never confused about the ownership of the garbage. Children called him Six-Ten. Not because of the timing of the school and absolutely not because of his height but his posture which with straight legs and straight bent torso, worn out by age, looked like ten minutes past six on the clock. With his conscientiousness the gatekeeper had marked defaulters and latecomers like Vicky and cursed them without missing a day, like a morning gratitude prayer. Six-ten saw Vicky approaching and started closing the gate. The faster he pedalled the faster he drew the gate and had almost closed the it by the time he reached. As he wriggled through Six-ten shook his head and sneered in his gruff voice, "Lazy latecomer!" Vicky was panting too hard to respond.

"Vicky licky why do you sweat like a pig all the time?" Aditya smacked hard at the back of his head and giggled. Rohit who stood behind Aditya sniggered. The prayer assembly was about to start.

"Chain got stuck in the flywheel...had to rush"

"Don't lie! You couldn't wake up on time. How many years since you took bath? You dirty fellow! You smell like a pig." Giggling Rohit squeaked so hard in his high pitch voice that everybody around started staring at them.

Aditya's and Rohit's devilry continued through the prayer. While others stood with their eyes closed and hands folded, they kept fidgeting, peeking around, inspecting others' faces body peculiarities, murmuring and giggling all the time. There was that defiance in their attitude which is so peculiar to adolescence of some individuals especially those with a compromised upbringing. Morning assembly over, the students started moving towards their classes. As they moved Aditya and Rohit pushed and shoved Vicky mocking him from behind. Vicky took everything in his stride. This was friendship between men.

Aditya and Vicky sat beside each other on the same bench, while Rohit sat immediately behind. Aditya's coarse behaviour grew out of conceit. Endowed with a tall athletic physique, spotless fair complexion and light brown eyes, he naturally drew attention of the adolescent girls around him. This automatically earned him the respect of boys. Younger son of an affluent industrialist, he was dropped to the school in a chauffeur driven imported car. Though he wore the same uniform, from his feet till the head, everything he adorned, carried the mark of exclusivity of his social class. To top it all, he was the topper of his class, for the last four years, all semesters continuously. With all these qualifications, for his young classmates, he was the living Greek God of beauty, wealth and success, all moulded into one and as he grew older he himself realised this even more. Though all his endowments were gradually getting overshadowed by his growing arrogance, selfishness and coarse vigorous mannerisms yet his conduct was tolerated by the naïve young students because irrespective of age or society, success defines what is right. Emboldened by his success and misled by the tolerance of others he had begun to putrefy in his privileges, rashly gravitating towards exhilaration provided by the abuse of substances, deviations of sex and adventures of scoundrels, like his new 'friend' Rohit.

Apparently, Rohit was Aditya's sidekick, but, in fact, he was the driving force behind Aditya's descent into wickedness. In appearance he was exactly the opposite of what Aditya was. When approaching from far his short, stout structure with a blunt face and a cunning smile gave the impression of an unkempt rogue waylaying passers-by. He was deviant and ill-disciplined and a constant source of consternation for the school as well as his parents. He was expert in sneaking away during school hours and had been caught by police once eve-teasing outside a girl's college. Many students had remarked a strange smell on him which many said was of cigarettes. But no body dared to challenge him. He had failed in his previous class and was repeating it. He was a rogue, senior to his classmates and made sure everybody remembered it.

Daily novelty of experience had attracted Aditya towards Rohit. Rohit was quick to gauge the opportunity and brought him to exciting experiences like cigarettes and porn on a regular basis. Too young to handle manipulations and sycophancy, Aditya thought that he had taken Rohit under his wings, unaware that rather he was Rohit's instrument. Together Aditya and Rohit were a team of wicked bullies of which Vicky was the third partner, by virtue of being Aditya's friend for the last nine years.

"OK everyone! Listen, listen, sit down you! pay attention!" Mrs Bunny, round and shrill, cried in her pleading high-pitched voice. She was loving and lenient and with her kindergarten attitude the class took liberties with her. "OK children! today you all have a new classmate who is joining you from..uh.. Modern right? As you can see she is an angel and don't you dare turn her into hobgoblins like yourselves." Everyone giggled. "Now please introduce yourself child!"

"My name is Sana Hussain. I am sixteen years old..."

"And! tell us about your parents, brothers and sisters, snow white! Miss Bunny interrupted.

"Sixteeeeeen! By God! what do they teach in bio? Tell me Ady?" Rohit whispered excitedly from behind. What's sixteen in that chapter of biology? Ady tell mee, I implore thee, heeheehee!"

Its not sixteen! Its between eleven to thirteen years, bloody failure! menstruation... puberty." Staring at the new entrant Aditya whispered back irritated.

I'm telling you Ady, she's is a pink fruit. ... I swear to God she has pink nipples! Oh my God! Help me! I'll die of erection." Aditya and Rohit started giggling.

As if an image had burst out of his heart and was now standing before him...alive. Overwhelmed Vicky was stupefied. He went numb, as if all his senses were focusing at just one point. Life around him vanished, unable to feel, hear or see anything other than the image that stood there...Sana.

"My father's name is Mr Abid Hussain. He is a teacher. My mother is a home maker. I have one younger sister Asma, who is in this school only, in class five."

"Ooo! I know that little sweet girl! Oh, what an angel! My God! you are her elder sister?... OK fine! Surabhi! just let her sit beside you. Help her and give her everything that has been taught till now! Classwork homework! Everything, Okay?"

As she passed by, Vicky had a fleeting sense that Sana had looked back at him and their eyes met for a moment but he wasn't sure. It had never happened before.

Slaaat! A hard smack from behind broke his reverie. "What are you staring at pig!" A hateful scowling smile contorted Rohit's face. Then he whispered to Aditya "She is sixteen, she is pink, knows everything, and is filled with unfulfillment...man its pouring from her eyes!" As he spoke Rohit looked at the sky with his eyes tightly closed."

Aditya giggled and then looked at Vicky. Vicky looked down adjusting himself on the bench.

Chapter Twelve

Holding the handmirror in one hand Vicky combed and settled his hair deliberately, taking his time getting ready for the school. Ashish seated on his chair was noticing his unusual behaviour.

"Aren't you little early?" Ashish asked.

"I want to leave early, don't want to rush every day."

"Wait! breakfast will take some time." Mother cried out from the kitchen.

As he pedalled along, a waft of the cool morning breeze passed his face gently. He slowed down, his breath normalised and he saw. A spectacular vista opened before him. The road flowed into a shallow bowl shadowed by the trees on both sides and then rising smoothly it disappeared beyond. Behind the spires and multi-storeyed buildings, the sun rose majestically. Bathed in orange the horizon awakened. Hymns arose from some temple far and interlaced with a koel's song resonated in the bowl. Columns of luscious green Eucalyptus along the road stood like humble priests swaying, singing, sparkling in lustrous glory. Dong! Proclaimed the bell in the church along the street. Dong! The vale reverberated. Vicky was pulled into a divine presence. Dong! Where had he been for so long? In his daily mad rush he had missed the most profound, that was always around. As he gradually rose up the road he breathed deeply as if to absorb the entire scene in his being.

Six ten was disoriented. He looked at his watch. Yet he wasn't sure. For the last three years, Vicky's arrival signalled the time to close the school gate. But today! He pulled one gate to close but he couldn't. Anxiously he looked at his watch again. There was still time. Vicky got down his bicycle casually and followed his curious eyes as he entered the school. He parked his bicycle in the parking stand and then wandered around the gate. 'Had she come? Would she come?' Every time there seemed a similar hair, or height or complexion his heart would jump out of its cage. As the time for the morning assembly drew closer his anxiety spiralled upto his chest. Six ten started to draw in the gates. He knew it was time for the morning assembly. Vicky's breaths went shallow. When the bell for the morning assembly whirred, his heart convulsed with pain. He could not bear to spend the entire day in that concentration camp without Sana. The gate closed. The students gathered and organized into assembly. Vicky remained standing facing the gate withering in the scorching sun.

"Vicky! Vicky!" Bawling Aditya came running and cracked him on his shoulders. "Are you deaf? Get back here. Can't you hear the bell? Vicky turned back. "What happ..." Vicky looked so sullen Aditya couldn't speak further. Vicky couldn't respond as well. He just went and stood in his class line.

"Vicky listen! I tell you dawg! Sana! Have you seen her you know...? like closely?" Aditya, standing behind Vicky whispered. Vicky was too dejected to say anything.

"Dawg! I saw her today from like this distance", Aditya put his palm in front of his eyes, she is ... Silk! I'm telling you!"

Taken aback Vicky turned back, "Today?"

"Yeah! Just now."

"Where?"

"In the class pig! Kept the bag, was coming out, she was coming in, almost banged into her! Wish I did! God! I'm so hard! It doesn't go! It's so hard it hurts!... AAh! ...I think I love her!"

"I didn't see her." Vicky tried to sound casual.

"Shut up man!"

"Shhh! Keep quiet children!" Mrs Bunny glowered.

Just then a voice arose "Our Father, who art in heaven..." and the combined voices of the children following the prayer rose like breaths of relief into the air. Vicky had never prayed with such gratitude.

In the coming months Vicky became an expert in finding and locating Sana. Pain had acquired him the skill. Both Sana and him sat horizontally apart on either side of the classroom. Vicky learnt to look at her while looking towards the teacher

151

in front. His peripheral vision expanded and zoomed to the extent that he could even see her nail polish from his seat. Stealing quick glances, he explored her deeply from every possible angle and absorbed each and every physical and behavioural nuance. Locked over her like a radar, he could locate her even among her clones. Yet, he wasn't sure whether she also noticed him, even though he felt it sometimes. But that was quite an impossibility. How could a girl like Sana like a sweating pig like him? He was satisfied with his modest achievements. As it is, it was unbearable to look at her full face. Once or twice, it had happened before and she had poured into his soul like molten metal and he couldn't sleep for days. His senses told him she was close by and that was enough.

It was ruckus. The Maths teacher had not come today and for some reason the substitute teacher couldn't make it as well. As the time passed chatter became commotion and commotion became chaos. The whole class broke into the cacophonous caw of a murder of crows fighting over a piece of meat. It was a zoo in disorder with all animals let lose on each other. Bullies like Rohit and Aditya pushed around other boys. Girls chatted away to glory or made faces at each other. The playful jumped over the benches and played hide and seek. Other threw fliers at each other. Vicky had become very conscious these days and satisfied himself with catching and collecting the fliers, taking advantage of the chaos to steal a look while Sana chatted with other girls enjoying her freedom as well. Soon all hell broke lose and the uproar got out of control.

"SHUT AAAAP ! Akha! Akha!" Mrs Bunny coughed. Her shrill voice gave way after hollering so loudly. "I wan't pin drop silence! Is this a fish market? What are you up to? and you Smita and you Vicky! What are you doing? What is that in your hand, a plane is it? Don't you have some shame? If there is no teacher in the class will you all become hooligaaaaans? Other teachers are saying what not about this class! And I have warned you again and again but you monsters are not willing to listen! Today I will teach every one a lesson. Till now I allowed you to sit with your friends on the condition that you'll behave. But instead you have relapsed into your Jurassic Kingdom. Enough is enough! Today I will change your seats. Nasir! Get up!...I said get up you dumbard! Pick up your bag! Fast! Come and sit near Loveleen. Surabhi! You go and sit near Rohit and heal his mind!" Aditya giggled.

Ady! You also get up. Go and sit near Rachna!" Rachna was the fattest girl in the class.

"Ma'm!... but there is no space there..." Aditya represented. Now Vicky giggled.

"SHUT AAAAP! do what you are told." Aditya picked up his bag and lumbered through the rows.

"Yeah, you Vijayant! Why are you laughing? What's the joke? What's so funny Hahn?"

"Yes, ma'am he is always talking", Rohit pranked hiding his grin.

"Shut up you Nin cum Poop! Am I talking to you? Vicky get up! Come and sit here, near Sana!"

The classroom murmur died immediately. Vicky's heart skipped a beat. Aditya mummified in his walk. Rohit, his eyes wide open, looked assassinated.

Vicky picked up his bag very softly. He didn't even want to breathe, lest Mrs Bunny change her mind. As he walked up cautiously through the silence, he could feel the cursing jealous breaths of his classmates warming up the air in the classroom. As he sat beside her he shivered with exhilaration. This pleasure had never passed his imagination. 'So this is heaven!' Still one question whispered in his head, 'Does Sana feel the same?'

"So? Have you started speaking to her?" Aditya asked looking askance at Vicky.

"What are you speaking to her?" Rohit cast a doubtful look.

"No I haven't." Vicky looked at them. Both Aditya and Rohit looked quite resentful. "You have a long way to go...dawg! You have to start speaking to her...then you have to make friends…. then you have to introduce me… then don't worry…. from thereon I will take over."

'Take over?' Vicky thought. 'Speak to her… Of course'

"Can I borrow your eraser?" Vicky could barely utter those words. He was trembling. 'Its over if she refuses. Might as well become a priest in this school itself!'.

Sana looked at him, opened her pencil box and gave the eraser to him, with a faint smile.

For the first time any girl had obliged and responded so easily without sneering. Even Surabhi, the most well-mannered girl in the class had been 'blank' with him. Yes, girls had shared their things before but not without an attitude. Her easy softness soothed him. 'Perhaps she is reflecting my feelings? Where did I read women can better sense the vibrations of people around them? So, she also likes me? Does she know what I feel about her? Shit man!' Nevertheless, when Sana gave the eraser, she at least had an understanding of a need and that was enough, understanding was enough. He was thankful. His feelings towards Sana started evolving.

Not a blemish of a cloud. The blue in the afternoon sky gleamed in a silverish lustre. In the shower of that effulgent warmth every speck bathed in light. The bell whirred, the sun glittered behind the spire and the children rushed out of their classes sparkling with joy. The school was over. Vicky stood leaning on his bicycle waiting to leave. The kids from the primary section were to clear up before the others could leave. His eyes wandered around warily. Behind him, the majestic church stood in the centre of a hollow square ground. On one side of the hollow square was the primary section and on the other side were the offices and the residence of the priest. The secondary section was a double storey behind the church. A passage ran alongside all the buildings. Just as he got ready to leave he saw Sana emerge from the shadow of the church walking so smoothly, as if she was floating. She came and stood under a shade in the passage along the primary section. Vicky's stomach dropped as if he was coming down a wheel swing. He forgot that he had to leave. He stood there feigning he was looking somewhere else while he furtively stole her glances. Standing in the shade was the slender ivory Goddess casually looking around. Suddenly she looked back at him. Like a divine light she radiated herself, came, fell upon him and embedded herself into his being. As if an elixir poured into him and Vicky drank it whole. By the time her school bus arrived, Vijayant was sozzled with Sana. His blood was full of her. Yet when she picked up her bag and walked outside, Vijayant acted hard that he hadn't noticed her. In this silent interaction, which barely lasted few moments, half an hour had passed in wonder.

Sana's school bus first brought some children from another school. Therefore, there was an interval between school getting over and the arrival of her bus. In the meantime, she waited in the passage of the primary section. It would have been foolish to share this information with Ady and Rohit.

Now Vijayant stopped rushing back home after the school. He wandered around the church, finding and hiding in some nook or corner and then peeking out just to steal Sana's final look for the day. Sometimes he would play with others who waited to be picked up after school. Sometimes he even felt Sana had caught him watching her. A shiver ran through his spine and he went and hid in some corner till his nerves calmed. Then he would come out again but find that she had already left, leaving him forlorn. He knew that it was strange that he sat with her the whole day and still he had to play this stupid hide and seek. He had all the opportunity to open up with her. But this matter was too sensitive for him. He did not want to be aggressive. He didn't want to be that Bollywood hero proclaiming his love on a loudspeaker on top of the college building. That would be stupid, embarrassing and would scare her off. He was also not sure about her feelings for him. What if she did not feel the same. Then what? What will she think of him? Lout? Predator? He still didn't know her fully. Who knows she might even go and complain and then Papa would kill him and then Ady and Rohit! They would kill him again! Could he confide his feelings to someone else? That would be 'Breaking News' for the whole world.

There was no one he could trust! It was best not to rock the boat at this time. Unable to express themselves, his thoughts, feelings and emotions further concentrated within.

"Where is Sana Vickyboy? Find her for me!" Aditya's behaviour was getting Vijayant on the edge.

In the recess Aditya, Rohit would take Vijayant to go around looking for Sana. Among the multitude of students wearing the same uniform it was difficult to locate her. But Vijayant was their Man Friday for this quandary. Even Vijayant loved testing himself on this challenge. After all his own interest was involved. Over a period of time, he had developed some kind of sensitivity for Sana. As he scanned the crowd his eyes and mind did some simultaneous calculations and suddenly it occurred to him that Sana should somewhere be at this and this location and when they went there most of the time, they would find her there to the wonder and jealousy of both his friends. But he felt that it was something else other than the eyes that helped him locate her. Maybe he was rising into some inexplicable dimension.

"There she is standing there, I think." Vijayant had brought them near the canteen.

"Wooah man!" Aditya exclaimed. "How did you know that! We were on the other side of the church!"

"He smelled her. He sits besidesher; he knows her smell. You really are a dawg after all!" Rohit sneered.

"Let's go there." Aditya spoke excitedly.

Both went and stood behind Sana. Vijayant remained behind, embarrassed and irritated.

Aditya went and stood close to Sana almost touching her and asked the shopkeeper, "How much is the sandwich?"

"Why sandwich? Buy me a lollipop." Standing audaciously at her breath's distance Rohit spoke loudly. Sana looked at them and then looked behind.

'Obscene!' Standing behind Vijayant turned red with embarrassment. He withdrew shamefully hoping to dissolve into the air.

Vijayant did not come from a privileged class like Aditya and Rohit. His middle-class background showed in the quality of his blazer, on the pale whiteness of his shirt, on the texture of his trousers, on the worn-out soles of his shoes, on his faded school tie, his torn up stitched again school bag and most importantly his dark complexion which was the very symbol of mediocrity in his society. Still, he made up for his drawbacks through his studies. In fact being Aditya's friend was a privilege granted to him because he was academically strong. Why was it like that? It is astonishing how various forms of classifications and stratifications come to be prevalent even in the innocent society of children as naturally and obviously as an inherent behavioural predilection. Students who are weak in studies are treated as inferior, students coming from wealthy families are seen as special. And that too by the children themselves! That too when the majority are average students from average backgrounds! The school is a sample of the utilitarian and exploitative nature of society. Society is ruthless with failures, weak and the poor. Just like animals. Look at the way dogs maul another injured mangy dog. Hatefully barking at him, biting, tearing up his wounds as if within them some maleficent devil resides that loathes the disadvantaged. Is human society any different? For all its ideals of liberty, equality and fraternity, how society still remains pack of wolves. It detests the vulnerable, segregates them, mistreats them, exploits them and abandons them. And it lies down, turns over meekly and surrenders itself to power. All its organization is just a hierarchy of privileges. This categorisation, stratification, and exploitation is not because of race or religion. It is a part of the animal in human. It can be subdued but it can never be eradicated. The sense of ownership of his 'friends' over Sana agitated Vijayant. They treated him as if he was just their agent. He dare not not even think of her! He was just a dog meant to smell her out for them??!!

"What happened?" Sana whispered.

The Social Science class was about to start. An irritated Vijayant was rummaging through his bag.

"I kept my Social Studies book in my bag in the morning…"

"We can share!"

Understanding! That's what she had, which nobody had had. Kind words dissolved in a mellifluous voice uttered from the tender lips of a rare beauty settled like a soothing balm over his burning heart. Vijayant stopped searching.

As both of them adjusted themselves to share the textbook he could feel the glare of burning eyes piercing the nape of his neck.

Chapter Thirteen

A brilliant vista lay before him. The church stood majestically in the centre. Hiding behind its spire, the sun sparkled occasionally. On the horizon the trees swayed ruffling their leaves lazily. Dong! And the kids scampered out of their classrooms. Laughing and running they came towards him but just as they reached him they burst into colourful petals. From the shadow of the church an orange butterfly emerged, its wings bordered intricately with gold swirls. It glided towards the passage beside the church, then swerved and wandered playfully towards him. It came closer and closer, floating around his face as if examining it closely. If he would just open his palms it would rest on it. But he dare not move, dare not speak, dare not breathe. He couldn't see what but something was holding him back and he was suffocating. Fluttering it held on. Finally taking a deep breath, with all his strength he raised his arm. Just then, it burst into sparkles. Dong!

Vijayant rose from the bed and walked upto the window. The moon was struggling to break out of the clouds. There had been a light shower. Down below the street was glimmering in the ambient light. The trees, glistening wet, stood absolutely still. A bat flew across from one shadow to the other playing seek and hide with the dark and the light. When he was in school he passed by this majestic hotel every day and wondered how would this street look from up there and how was the horizon. Now he was there. It was an observer's perspective indeed. From the window he could see himself standing in the dark street looking back at himself standing at the window. 'I am He and He is I'. On the horizon he could see a light blinking on a cross, atop the spire of the church. His school.

Vijayant and Sana started noting a compatibility between themselves. There was an unsaid understanding of the need of the other. Similar tastes, likes and dislikes, pleasures and anxieties. School had been an anxious harsh place for Vijayant but ever since Sana had come life had become so serene. Vijayant did not expect Sana to open up so easily to him. She was reserved and hardly interacted much with anyone except Surabhi and Rita Gupta. Boys were out of question. But with him! Sometimes in casual group interactions he felt that she was biased towards him. How come? He had not even told himself that during classes Sana reclined her knees upon his legs while she was sitting beside him. Did she know it or did she do it unconsciously? All these years everyone had always made him feel that he was quite ordinary. And now Sana! the most extraordinary splendour in the school, whom even boys from other classes were trying to approach, was treating him 'specially!'

Vijayant even developed a scientific theory behind her affability towards him. This was : Humans are electromagnetic systems with their respective polarities. Say, women are negative poles and men are positive. Female and male gender of a species have fundamentally opposite polarities. But polarities are not simply positive and negative. In case of complex beings, like humans, the polarity varies in shades i.e., intensity, between the negative and positive. Say some men are less positive while some women tend more towards the negative domain of polarity. It is the degree of oppositeness of polarity between two complex beings that determines the intensity of attraction. The more opposite the polarity the stronger the attraction. And where does this polarity come from? It is the product of the body's chemo-bio-physical system, including the gene. Not to forget, society and environment which also have an effect on the psychological biases. But polarity is provincial, limited to the species concerned. A normal man is not sexually attracted to say, spiders. There lies the role of genes. Inference? He and Sana had extreme opposite polarities. Enjoying the mornings and afternoons while cycling back and forth to school Vijayant would dwell and condense his vague ideas into theories and theories into philosophy, then laughing upon himself he would ask, 'Otherwise why would she love me?... ... ...But does she love me?'

"You know why you don't have a girl friend?" Rohit asked in his usual mocking tone.

"Why?" Vijayant responded casually.

"Because you are ugly!" Rohit threw his punch line and then both Aditya and Rohit giggled.

Then Aditya said, "Because you don't have the... the.. the what to say... the temperament of a lover."

"Well expressed! I must say sir!", said Rohit with a sneer. Vijayant remained silent.

"Today is Valentine's Day." Aditya said.

Vicky gave puzzling look. "I don't have any..."

"But I have...and you know who."

Vijayant looked perplexed. Aditya held forth a card at him.

"Open it! Oopen!"

Vijayant opened the card and a romantic instrumental started playing.

"This is a musical card." Aditya said proudly.

Vijayant found it enchanting. He opened and closed the card repeatedly and every time he opened the card the music played.

"Stop! Battery will go down!"

"How much?" Vijayant asked examining the the card

"One twenty."

"One twenty!! You bought a card for one twenty rupees!! Where did you get that kind of money?"

"One twenty is not much. Now shut up and listen! This is for Sana but probably she knows today is Valentine's Day and has gone into hiding somewhere."

"She knows everything." Rohit said taking a deep breath.

"But she was here only, all morning! Why would she come to school if she had to go and hide somewhere?"

"Then arrange a meeting with her. I want to give her this card."

"Are you mad! I can't do this ! What would she think of me!"

"Wow!! What about what would we think of you?" Rohit said.

"Vicky listen! we have been friends for years...", Aditya warned him. Rohit smirked. "People vouch by our friendship. You are my man! Won't you help your brother in a matter which concerns his life? His soul?" Vijayant looked on aghast. "Vicky I really like Sana; it is not sexual... it is more than that. And I need you! You have to do this... ... bro!!" He added the last word after some thought.

"This is not a movie Ady!"

"Go and talk to her. God has made you sit over there so that you can be my path to her."

"I don't know where she is."

"You always know Vicky, you always know where Sana is, don't you??" Aditya said. "I am telling you if you are my true friend and a man, get her to me... before this interval gets over... just ten minutes left. Go!"

Inadvertently Aditya forgot to take back his card. Vijayant walked off bewildered, holding the card in his hand. How could he say anything like that to Sana. Today was Valentine's Day! Why would he approach Sana for someone else? His mind went hazy and everything started blurring out. Dawdling he reached the corner of the corridor where a few vague figures appeared.

Sana and Surabhi approached from the other side. Sana's eyes wandered towards his hand. She slowed down and looked strangely into his eyes. But Vijayant was too dazed to say anything. As she passed by he muttered, "Sana!"

"Vijayant!" Sana responded instantly.

"Sana... ....Ady wanted to talk to you."

"For?" When she looked slightly askance her pupil shifted to the corners of her eye. It was then Vijayant realized how shapely her eyes were and they looked right into his soul. Approaching Sana for someone else! He felt like weeping.

"I don't know...I don't know ...wants to give you a gift or something." Vijayant looked down at the card in his hand, shamefully.

"What does he want?" Sana was irked for a moment but then she looked at Vijayant's face and said "OK I'm waiting here." Surabhi giggled.

Aditya and Rohit walked up like criminals rising the gallows. Vijayant pale with shame, led them, holding the card like his own sentence. All three came up stood in front of her. Rohit poked Aditya but he couldn't utter a word. Sana looked straight at Aditya. Without his self- styled confidence, he looked quite ordinary.

Sana waited a while for Aditya to say something. Then she said in a firm voice, 'I can't take this…" She thought for a moment and then spoke again, "What if someone sees all this. People will talk about me! What if Mrs Bunny comes to know, then?"

"Then let's us get over with it fast!" Vijayant held forth the card straight towards Sana. It was another way of destroying himself - Fast.

In a snap of a moment Sana took the card from Vijayant's hand and then it vanished. Everything happened so quickly everyone was stunned! Only Rohit looked on suspiciously. Suddenly the bell rang and the girls began to walk away.

"Wai wai wait …please!" Rohit said.

"What now!" Aditya whispered annoyingly.

He showed his right hand. It was a small camera. "Let's click a photograph…. …to mark in our memories the beginning of a long-term relationship…God bless Saint Valentine!" He tried to sound enthusiastic. The girls looked on awkwardly. "Vicky just click a photograph!"

"Are we going to get a copy?" Surabhi asked coyly.

"Of course!" Rohit smiled confidently.

Vijayant kept mulling over what had happened and what it meant. From what was apparent it seemed Sana did not like Aditya. Thank Goddess! But did she like him? He did not want to take any chances with her. If she refused, he would just break up and scatter. He didn't have the courage to face that consequence. Over the last few months, she had become the centre of his life. He could not get her out of his mind. All his thoughts and actions revolved around her. As if she had been stamped onto his brain. As this happened, he became more and more aloof, even from Aditya and Rohit. What was the point? He couldn't share his feelings with anyone specially with them. Conflict of interest. But the quieter he grew, richer grew his inner world. Society had enchained his thought to think of life only in terms of success and failure, gain or loss. His approach towards life was utilitarian. Life was suffering. But when Sana touched his soul, a sense of beauty came over him. He felt the world more deeply. The gravity and the serenity of the trees, the cool freshness of the morning breeze, the warmth of the rising sun, the night ornamented with stars, and the deep pleasure of longing in the silence of the night! Now he was seeing! Now he was feeling! Now he was awake!!

The bright confidence of getting his card accepted was gradually being shadowed by dark clouds of doubt in Aditya's mind. 'Why didn't she accept the card from my hand? Oh! there was no time. She must be a little shy. She almost snatched the card from Vijayant's hand! Oh! she knows him by now. She must be more confident about him. Does she like him? Vijayant! That Vicky! Kallu(Blackie)!. That black sweaty pig! no way!'

Sana was not at her place right now. Vijayant noticed a chit lying inside her pencil box. There was something written on it. It was a common practice to stick your name and address slip on the pencil box just in case if it was mixed up or misplaced it could be traced and returned. He looked around nervously to see if anyone was watching, and then noted down the details on that slip.

Vijayant did not return home after school. He waited a while after Sana left and then started for her house. He didn't want Sana to know he was following her. The road led to the old city. Lined by medieval era parks, monuments and mosques and covered by archways of a unique architectural style, the road looked like the gateway to the past. He had seldom been to this part of the old city. It was like a treasure hunt. He was gasping with excitement. Groups of people wearing skull caps passed by. Most of the women wore burquas or covered their heads. This was predominantly and evidently a Muslim area. He had heard that the old city was quite congested and chaotic. It didn't seem so. Compared to the crowded fast paced city centre there were far less people on the streets. He had to ask around to locate the obscure lane where her house was situated. In uniform, some people doubted him while others were concerned, he had forgotten his way. At last, by late afternoon he was able locate the lane. He parked his bicycle on a side and walked down cautiously looking out for any danger. At the end of the street, a little separated from the line of other houses was an old heritage bungalow. It was walled around, therefore he could hardly see anything inside. But from the façade and style it was clear that this structure was more in consonance with the medieval architecture he had noticed on the main road than the other houses on the same street. While his heart pounded his chest, he walked up closer to the entrance. Two cars stood in the garage inside. Some fellows wearing skull caps were working in the garden. The whole place had a traditional aura about it. Suddenly, a worker looked towards the gate where he was standing. Startled he turned about immediately. It was suicidal to be conspicuous. Even Sana might be offended, if she came to know. He had found the place where she lived. This was enough. "When Columbus discovered America even he didn't know how big it was going to be. It is just the beginning yet it is an achievement indeed!' He wanted something. He had done something about it. Filled with warm contentment he walked back to his bicycle. As he cycled back home he felt hungry but barely any shops were open.

Vijayant had already woven his answers when he reached home. Calmly responding to every predictable rapid-fire question with genuine lies he went on with his things. Then he retired to his own corner with his books leaving his parents wondering about his amiability.

"School closing from tomorrow?" Ashish asked.

As if an arrow pierced his heart, "No! why! What happened?"

"I thought they were closing from tomorrow? Not yet?"

"Noo! Why?"

"Same old Hindu-Muslim, what else? Good for you people, holidays now. Enjoy!"

"We haven't been told anything!" Vijayant replied excitedly. "Very important classes running now, can't miss them."

"You mean you want to go to school? Everything OK?"

A procession carrying orange and red triangular flags passed by shouting slogans, beating drums, and banging plates and utensils.

"Ram lalla ham ayenge, Mandir wohinbanayenge!" (O Lord Rama! we will come and build the temple over there.)

He had been seeing these processions for some time but now the number of people had gone up significantly. Even women and children were participating in the processions. There were barricades that had come up at every other place and the policemen were deployed all over.

"We will have the temple, no matter what! It was always there." Rohit whispered excitedly. "Do these hypocrites mean to say that that barbarian Babar built a mosque on some vacant piece of land in the birthplace of Lord Rama?" Aditya and other boys listened on while the muslim students sat murmuring in the other corner.

But Vijayant and Sana remained indifferent to the prevailing madness. They sequestered themselves far from this madding crowd in their tender serene reality.

"Where do you stay?" Sana whispered.

"Cantonment. You?"

"Old city. Have you been there?"

Vijayant was stumped. Had she seen him? Was this a question or a suggestion? He did not want to lie to her and he could not find any other excuse. He just mumbled something

"Sana!" The Maths teacher walked in for the class, "Why isn't your work complete?"

"Mam! I ... I was absent on that day."

"So what! You got to complete your work! Complete it! Submit, tomorrow!" Sana sat down nervously.

In the break Vijayant offered his notebook promptly, "My work is complete. Copy it from mine."

"How will I copy here? Classes are going on !"

"Then you take it home!"

173

For the first time Vijayant discovered any practical use of completing his homework on time. Years of work in that mosquito filled corner had finally borne fruit. More than that when his copy would be returned it would bear her touch and her scent. He just couldn't wait for his notebook to return duly adorned. But there was something more. For the first time he had discovered the joy of giving which the school brother kept talking about. 'The giver should be as thankful as the receiver' It was true indeed! But when you give to someone as an expression of your love and its accepted-It's a prayer realized.

"Tomorrow is PT test!" Sana smirked. She looked even more beautiful that way.

"Everyone passes PT", VK said casually. "No marks are even given for it, only A B C."

"It is difficult only for me."

"Why?"

"Because my father is the PT teacher."

Vijayant almost jumped on the bench, "Hussain sir is your father?"

Sana nodded guiltily

"Even I'll fail today. I can't remember the routines anymore." Vijayant mumbled. When he turned his head he saw Sana giggling away.

"Somebody beat you?" Rohit asked.

"Are you mad!" Aditya was offended by the question.

"Then what are you brooding about?... Sana?"

"What !!" Aditya turned red.

"Sana ...And Vicky...and he was your last man standing!" Aditya looked on blankly. "I don't understand how a girl like Sana would love that ugly black pig."

"Girls love who they sense loves them more. They are not same as us...we want to possess they want to be possessed." Aditya spoke in a thoughtful tone.

"Wooh! That was deep. But you're right, probably your aura is weak therefore Sana couldn't feel it. Therefore, your best friend, whom you employed to find your way to Sana, could hijack her for himself. Still, it is betrayal! You don't do that. You don't do that between brothers! Imagine Sana has preferred a mediocre like him over you! I just can't take this!" Rohit kept rubbing it in. "And you...you like a fool were so happy when that polar bear Bunny made him sit near Sana!"

Aditya remained silent but his expressions were changing.

"And you will tolerate this? The whole class knows Sana was perfect for you. They are laughing behind your back."

His nostrils swollen, Aditya was breathing heavily now and his jaws crushed against each other,

Satisfied his words had made an impact, Rohit spoke in a malicious strain, "Calm down! Why harm him when you can hurt him."

175

"What are you even talking about, psycho?" Aditya scowled.

A hateful cruel sneer drew across Rohit's face.

"Come here, You!" Mr Abid Hussain called out in a rough voice, pointing with his fingers. The class was had fallen in rows for PT.

"Yes, you! What's your name?"

Vijayant tried to avoid looking at him. 'You bet someone told him I had gone to their house. O God! He's not calling me?'

"Yes, I am calling you only! Come here."

Vijayant gave up. He started walking up to the teacher. His crime had been discovered and now he was going to be brought before everybody, humiliated and thrown out of the school... and then he would never see Sana ever again! With that thought he felt his heart burst and blood splattered across his eyes. Vijayant stood in front of Mr Hussain shoulders drooped.

"What is this?"

'What is he asking? Is there something on me?' Vijayant was confused as he inspected himself.

"Yes! This! what is this strand you are wearing on your hand"

"This?"

"Yes this thread", there was an angry irritated look on Mr Hussain's face.

'Thank God! Holy mother of cow!' Relieved, Vijayant breathed out heavily. "Sir Sacred thread!

176

Actually yesterday evening we went to the temple. There the priests tie it on everyone's hand. It's auspicious." He spoke cheerfully with a childlike innocence while Mr Abid stared at him.

After he finished there was a momentary silence and then Mr Hussain said sharply, "Go back!"

Though taken aback, he was still relieved. 'How can he not be aware of this?', he wondered as he returned to his row.

Even though they were mostly around each other both the guessing lovers had been avoiding eye contact. A direct look would pierce right through their heart and the wound would never heal. Yet their heart craved that most painful pleasure.

Rita was the most attractive girl in the class after Sana, though much less desirable because the class thought she was a little 'off', like she would start crying if the electricity went off and the fan stopped working or she would belch like a tyrannosaurus after tiffin, etc. There was no problem with her. She was a pampered and only child of rich parents. But these days she had gone mad. A senior in the intermediate, who obviously didn't know her peculiarities, wrote her a love letter. It was written in blood. Mighty impressed by the Christ like sacrifice made for her she pranced around whispering her secret to her select few-The entire class. Turns out the letter was written in the frog's blood that was dissected in the biology lab the previous day. And what made it even more gross was that she had been gloating all over it smelling, kissing and licking it lovingly all day-Again secretly. When she came to know the truth the chubby cute girl transmogrified into a Queen Kong. Though she was recovering now, she was still emotionally tentative making people around her a little anxious. The seat behind Sana and Vijayant was vacant today. For some reason known only to her she got up from her usual seat and came and sat immediately behind Sana and Vijayant making them anxious as well.

It was the mathematics period. Both the teacher and the topic were intense. Except the teacher everyone else was quiet, totally engrossed. Suddenly Rita squealed. Startled Vijayant and Sana look back simultaneously. It was nothing- Rita bit her nails too deep. Relieved they began to turn back ahead but the moment their heads turned, their eyes met and couldn't move further.

'Studies! Job! Unemployment! Muslim! Parents! Marriage! Sex! Wrong! Ady! Wrong thing!'

In that moment of quintessential experience his rationality bombarded Vijayant's heart with all its insecurities. Sana stood at the threshold of his life asking to come in but Vijayant blinked and looked down. The moment had passed.

Vijayant knew immediately that whatever happened was cataclysmic. His heart sank. As he cycled back home the world seemed lifeless as before. Home was the same sweaty corner. He had made a rational choice and now everything seemed rational. Dry and dead. His soul was restless. Something was withering inside.

"Sana!" Mr Abid Hussain shouted even before he could enter the house. Alarmed that something was wrong, his wife and Asma (Sana's younger sister) sitting in their bedroom stood up. "Where's Sana?" He hollered. He was sweating. Sana's mother stood gasping while Asma looked for somewhere to disappear. "Sanaaa!" he went about shouting looking into the other rooms. Suddenly he noticed a shadow in the verandah standing upfront, full face, watching like the dead.

"I'm calling you! Cant you hear?"

Sana remained silent, still. 'No response! Such obduracy! insult!'

Mr Abid spoke in a cold voice. "Get your school bag."

Mr Abid snatched the bag from her hands and turned it over. The bag was full. Everything started falling out. He scanned all the stuff scattered around. It wasn't there. He held forth the bag to return. Just as she raised her hand to take it back, Mr Abid retracted and just to confirm, jerked it harder, .

A card fell on the ground. Everyone looked on stunned. For a moment it lay there lifeless, then its upper leaf quivered and lifted slightly and the music started playing. Sana's father looked as if someone had just run a sword across his back.

Chapter Fourteen

Communal tensions flared up. A man was killed in the old city and sporadic rioting was reported. The class was rejoicing. There being likelihood of more riots the district administration had ordered the schools to shut down from the next day. Holidays had been declared and the semester exams had been postponed, indefinitely. Sana had not been coming to school for the last three days and now holidays. Vijayant was withering like a lonely seedling in the desert. Yet he assured himself.

'She lives in the old city. Riots there! How would she come? Max a week and they will open the school again. They can't live without killing us with tests. Why hasn't she come?... ... Will she come?'

The school did open... after a fortnight. But Sana didn't come.

"Where's Sana? Why isn't she coming to school, Vicky?" Cold revenge dripped from Rohit's salivating smile.

Vijayant shook his head. He noticed that Rohit had called him Vicky. Normally he would call him a pig or a dawg. Aditya stood directly behind Vijayant sniggering.

"How come? You can sense her! You can pull her from anywhere! Why can't you get her here?"

Then pointing towards Aditya he said. "See my friend is dying. Do something, Vicky!"

"Go away!" Vijayant snapped.

"Maybe she is preparing for exams!" Aditya said in a patronizing tone masquerading as a well-wisher.

"Which exams? Have the dates come?" Rohit asked.

"No!" Aditya said, "...or maybe she is not well or something! Why would someone just leave school mid-session...only if there is something seriously wrong... grave mistake...like...like shameful..." He looked askance at Vijayant trying to guess if he felt guilty for betraying his friend. "Am sure there is nothing like that...She is going to come you'll see!"

What's better than killing the enemy softly, with hope. Aditya and Rohit relished every sip of their cold sweet revenge.

Vijayant was worried. Things did not feel the same anymore. As if some astral alignment had been disturbed when he blinked that day. As if at that moment he was at the crossroads of space-time where he had to make a choice. He had made it. He had chosen logic over love. And now his life was exploding in that direction like a fission chain reaction hurtling away from his previous existence astronomically. He knew what Aditya said about her possible return was not true, yet he wanted to believe it. As if belief would pull Sana out from the vanishing oblivion. But the moment was gone.

Why did he make that choice? Why was he so cautious or as they say 'rational'? Because this trepidation had been ingrained into him by his parents, society, education. He had been programmed into thinking the way he thought... by his environment. Instead of accepting life with open arms, he had been taught to save himself from it. Was he actually 'rational'? He was too young to understand that what we think is rationality is limited by our knowledge, perception and understanding. Beyond this rationality lies the rationality of the universe containing infinite invisible threads connecting one thing to another in a manner that is far beyond the apprehension of our reasoning process. Yes, it can be apprehended in a moment by a sense that some call intuition. But few are that sensitive. Rather we are numbed by our beliefs, deluded by our thoughts, and irrationalized by our rationality. Within him there was someone who wanted the truth but it had been subdued to the extent that even its screaming cries remained voiceless. Vijayant had abandoned his soul for his mind and now he must live the hell.

'Till now I have always asked you for good marks and a government job. But God! today I take back all my demands.' With his eyes pressed tightly and hands clenched hard Vijayant prayed desperately, murmuring his pain with his puckered lips. He had left home for college but was too uneasy to go there. So he came to the temple to seek redress and relief. While he prayed hard, many stared at him, rightly suspicious that he had missed school since he was in uniform. 'Please forgive me and grant me Sana…everything else I would make possible…I'll live in poverty but If I don't get Sana I will live like dead. Oh my lord! grant me Sana and I ask nothing else!'

At the culmination of his prayer, he went round the *sanctum sanctorum*. As he walked around his eyes fell on the walls of the gallery. Millions of wishes were scribbled on them. Desires and desperations written with nervous pleading hands, threads and cloths, hopes and cries tied to the grills. What he would have irritably dismissed as superstition previously, in his own desperate times, seemed reasonable. 'Maybe they have some effect'. What seems superstition to some is the only way out for the desperate. Again he was too young to know that God, religion, and faith are themselves testimonies of the desperations and desires of man. Through the ages, with such helplessness has man stood against his circumstances that only a miracle could save him.

"Can I have my maths classwork back?" Vijayant asked hesitantly.

"Of course! you should have taken it long back." Rohit flipped the copy on the desk, "Can't copy that much as it is. So much bullshit they teach in class and ask barely ten in the exams."

"Rohit you remember on Valentine's Day you had clicked a photograph of all of us?" Rohit's raised his eyebrows. Vijayant could barely meet Rohit's eyes. "You said everyone would get a copy."

"You remember you clicked the photo?" Rohit's tone suddenly changed, "So you are not in there, then what do you need the photo for?"

"Oh yes! Right." Mortified, Vijayant retreated abruptly.

Sitting a few rows behind Aditya saw, Vijayant sitting alone, in one corner of the bench, given adequate space to the other side, as if Sana would come and sit anytime. A lonely supplicant, head slightly bent, in his prayer, silent, turbulent, and he felt tearing up inside.

Days turned into months but instead of receding, Vijayant's sentiments grew even stronger. Sana was gone yet she remained, in his being-as a sensation. In every face, he sought her face, in every feeling he craved her feel. Every day, after school, he would wait at the gate, glancing at the passage, anxious that Sana might emerge from the shadow, walk up to the passage, and look back at him. But it didn't happen. Then he would go home disappointed, yet hopeful. Sometimes he would wander in the church's cool shadow, where she stood. The passage beside the church became his shrine. Every morning became hope, every day a penitence, every night a prayer and he, a recluse.

"My dear Children, today we have gathered here to bid farewell to our students of class twelfth." The principal's lofty voice resounded the auditorium. "Most of you have spent many years in this school. Rather, since childhood you've spent most part of your days here. School has been your life and let me tell you, you have been the life of this school. But today the day has come when you must go forth into the world. For education, you gave yourself unto us and through education we gave ourselves unto you and education will give you the strength and the capability to meet all the challenges that you face in life. Though it brings sorrow, separation teaches us. It teaches us the transience of time and the impermanence of everything. A consciousness of impermanence reminds us of the value of every moment and everything but at the same time detaches us from them."

"What is he talking about?" A student whispered to the other.

"Is it going to come in the boards?"

"Where do you get that weed?" Another enquired.

"So, as you leave us do not be sad. For we are always with you, in you, through our education. We may have passed from your sight but we remain in you. As you step out of the gates a new world opens in front of you. Open your heart and go forth! Farewell!"

The auditorium rose in applause. The lights came on. The students moved to the quadrangular garth beside the auditorium decorated with lights for the farewell celebrations. As the evening set in the enclosure glowed in the soothing yellow light and a warm love filled the sorrowful air of separation. Dancing, embracing, laughing, crying, excited, scared every heart opened up to soak up the last drop of their sweet childhood. The universe spoke to Vijayant through the principal beckoning him to the present. Indifferent, impervious, impuissant, Vijayant's mind couldn't pull itself out of oblivion.

With every day of Sana's absence, Vijayant slid a little more down a dark abyss. The sun, the breeze, the chirps, the trees, first everything became meaningless and then invisible. Every day the sap of life within him dried a little more, finally detaching from the world like a leaf fallen off from a tree. He forgot time and time forgot him. Shrivelling and curling into himself, slowly he grew invisible like the wind, unseen but carrying a storm in its heart.

"Why have you screwed your pre boards?" Holding the result in his hand Ashish asked piquantly.

Vijayant was drawing. He didn't bother to look up.

"Your boards are a month away, when your performance should be peaking you are…"

"Performance!!!…Am I a horse?"

"Here you have to perform to survive with dignity fool!" Ashish shouted, "You know what is the employment scene in India? What will be your future? You'll crawl like a worm!"

Vijayant raised his burning eyes and then asked coldly, "Why did you give birth to me?"

"Whaat!"

"If you're so worried about my future why did you give birth to me???"

"Are you mad!"

"You keep talking about the employment sceeeene all the time! It has been like this in India forever. This is not new. Before having sex with mother were you not aware that a child would be born and you will have to look after his future? Still you produced me and now you keep lecturing me on the employment sceeeeeeeeene all the time! If you were so worried about it you should have controlled yourself! I am the embodiment of your sin!" Vijayant had emerged from his corner and now stood in the centre of the room.

"Shut up Vicky! Why do you talk so weirdly!" Suchitra said at the threshold of the kitchen.

"You bought me to this hell!! When you were rubbing your body against her what was the amploymentsceeeene!"

188

Suddenly Vijayant felt a strong blow on his face, his head hit the bed and he fell on the floor. Ashish had slapped him hard.

"Noooo!!!!" Suchitra cried and rushed to pick him up.

"Don't you get out of your boots. Whatever we are saying is for your own good." Scowling with disgust, holding his palms in his hand, Ashish exited immediately.

The board result was as expected. Vijayant was neither surprised nor bothered. He felt too broken and scattered to concentrate on anything. His mind had wandered off into some wilderness and all this seemed meaningless. Worse was the indifference of his parents. Already been forewarned by his attitude they accepted his downfall as destiny. With his performance, he could only manage an admission into a mediocre college.

A facility available easily is not regarded as a privilege. Vijayant had been studying at St Joseph's Senior Secondary since nursery. In his conception that's how all schools were. He never realized that he had had the privilege of studying in one of the most renowned schools in the state. In that compact controlled secure environment, all the flowers had grown like in a well-tended garden. But this college was a weed-infested undergrowth. Everything from infrastructure to education was in decadence. In the name of freedom, chaos prevailed. Most of the boys were sexually frustrated and desperate. The girls also behaved oddly as if they had been abandoned in a forest full of hungry wolves, true to a great extent. Everything from their thoughts to conversation to manners was strange. To him, it was a disorderly rabble. Unable to adjust to the alien environment Vijayant retracted to his old habitat.

Just to assure his parents, every morning he left home in time for the college, but instead he went to Sana's bungalow. Discreetly standing somewhere he waited, hoping to catch just a glimpse of her some day. Sana could never be seen, though in a few days, people around began to grow suspicious. To avoid trouble he moved farther away wandering alone aimlessly in various quarters of the old city. But in the afternoon, he would surely reach his old school around the time it got over and stand outside, a little away from gate, watching over the passage beside the church where Sana came and waited for her bus. Then once every student had left, he would depart disappointed, yet hopeful that one day or the other Sana would at least come to visit her old school and then she would find him there. In his religiosity he had refused to take cognizance that ever since Sana had stopped coming to school, even Mr Abid Hussain had not been seen.

His routine became a ritual. Daily he would leave home in the morning, wander around for a while, then around afternoon he would go to school. There he would stand a little far from the gate from where he could watch over the passage discreetly. Then after everyone had left and there was no hope of Sana he would return, hopeful for the next day, satisfied that he had paid his penitence. Many times, as he stood there one of his old classmates would pass by. He would either not recognize them or avoid them, or hide somewhere or walk away or just ignore them straightaway. All measures to avoid the consciousness lurking within, breathless with a question. Its not easy to know, when to hold on, when to let go. When Sana stood at the threshold his heart, asking to come in, his rationality withheld him. But now that she was gone, his rationality also abandoned him. On the foundation of his loss Vijayant built his card-temple of hope and locked himself in it.

Hi Vicky!"

'Teacher! Caught!' Vijayant just froze where he stood. 'Should have changed the place, now complaint...principal...police...yaaaaaaaqh! Can't even do nothing...why? am I harming them? NO! Can't I even stand here?'

"Vicky! Vicky! hello!"

'Wait! is that ...' "Surabhi?"

"Yes ! why were you scowling?"

"I thought you were a teacher!"

"What!"

"What are you! I mean where are you these days." Vijayant had to stress hard to find what to say.

"First ask how are you."

"Oh! How are you."

"I am fine. I am in Loreto! What about you?"

"I am in Ramakant."

" Bio? "

"No!!."

"Ok Maths?"

"No, Humanities." Embarrassed he looked down.

"Oh!", A disappointed smile drew across her face. "Change of plans? But that is also good. How come you are here?" Her penetrating eyes demanded the truth.

"I was just passing by...with a friend. He is somewhere around." Vijayant looked around feigning he was looking for that friend.

"I am with my friend too! She has come to pick up her younger brother today...You don't look like you ever left the school! I also feel that way. Can't ever forget those days...can we? You remember when Aditya came with a card....You saw his face??" She chuckled

"Oh yeah! Those days!" Vijayant wondered whether she had already forgotten those days and remembered it only today when she saw him, as if she had seen a ghost from the past.

"Where are they...Ady went to Mumbai I know! Rohit failed!" She giggled "I wonder what he is doing now? And Sana...?"

Now it was Vijayant's turn to give a penetrating look.

Suddenly, Surabhi looked behind. "Ok my friend is calling me. I have to leave. Came here after so long and found you here, at the same place! It was great to meet you. Wish we could get back."

Vijayant just nodded absentmindedly, confused what to say. In the absence of society he had forgotten all the social clichés. As she departed Surabhi looked at him curiously.

'She looked like ...a grown-up woman.' As he cycled back home Vijayant recollected that both his and Surabhi's birthday fell one day after the other. 'How much older than me? Not much, between people in the same class?'

Chapter Fifteen

The sun had set. The sky was still in flames. A shadow loomed around the school gate.

'Six ten!!' Vijayant squinted to focus. No! must be dead by now. Gone! Not stuck ...like me...much time has passed!' Vijayant stood on the threshold of the school gate as if on the boundary of two time zones. "Today is Sunday, wont the church be open for a while?" He enquired.

The gatekeeper stood still for a moment then stood aside as if he was guarding the entrance to a surreal world. Vijayant stepped in with a thundering heart. As he walked towards his shrine he felt being pulled into the eye of the firestorm.

"What's going on?"

Vijayant had returned after his daily ritual. It was already late afternoon. Things were lying all over. Two-three labourers were hauling and arranging boxes. Another was gathering the scrap lying around and piling it up in a pyre. Ashish looked back and ignored him and continued directing the workers.

"Told you to pack up your things! Why haven't you?" Suchitra yelled.

His face did not betray the dark hole whirling in his stomach. His mother had been talking about it the whole time but he had ignored it. They were tenants here. Now his father had made his own house and they were moving out. They were leaving. But he had spent his entire childhood here! It meant much more to him than a house. This was his home. Time was moving like a tornado extirpating his world from its roots.

"Did you pack my notebooks...were kept on the book shelf?" Vijayant's voice shivered.

"All those were of the last year, we won't carry any garbage!"

Suddenly he heard a crackle and turned back. A labourer had ignited the pyre of scrap. His father was standing by. A strong breeze blew across and the blaze rose fiercely. Unmindful Vijayant walked up close. So many things that were so much part of his everyday were now in the pile of junk crowned with all the small little treasures of his childhood. His world was on fire. Celebrating the destruction, a few children cavorted around. Suddenly, toppled by the violent sways of the flame, a burning notebook slid down towards the side, pages fluttering, flipping over, over and over, sketches of Durga, burning away from the corners, images of Durga, pages flipping over, images of Sana, images of Sana breaking up into embers, blowing away. With a voracious grunt the fire lapped up everything. Then, in a final swathe it proclaimed all its peripheral possessions before settling down on its dark smouldering throne. Stunned, Vijayant stood gazing into the apocalypse.

It was getting dark when he regained his senses. People had got on with their life after the small celebration and the gathering had dispersed. Vijayant, still confounded, turned and went inside. The room was empty. In the absence of everything home was a tomb. In a corner lay a pile of disposables. On it reclined a book size square wooden board. Nervously he moved up, sat down on his haunches, picked it and turned it over. The face of Durga. The face to which he had opened his eyes every morning and the eyes which had put him to sleep every night, the mother under whose watchful eyes he had grown up, lay there face fallen, deposed disposed, nose broken. As if some arrangement of the mind shattered. The mother was no more, the home had broken. Amongst the remnants lay the hand mirror - glass split. His broken self looked back at him. Behind, he could see in the mirror, time, the darkness smothering the evening, gaping through the window approaching him.

Vijayant stood in the darkness like a soul unreleased. The spire of the church had dissolved into the darkness. Against the sprawling mantle of the night the great white statue of Christ, on the façade of the church, in its flowing robe, floated in serene luminosity, both hands spread as if proclaiming 'Let there be light!' A tear rolled down the corners of his eyes, grimacing he cried out a sigh. 'Why?'

From the depth millions of pictures burst forth, floated up and rose up to his eyes. Each picture a memory, a sensation, an essence.

Waiting for Sana-Hopeful anxiety: Her sudden absence-Terrible distress: Processions marching by-Curious fear: Rohit's scornful face-Disgust: After school hide and seek -Nervous pleasure: The road-Breezy serenity: Father-Selfish Parsimony: His study table-Home: Burning flipping Durga, Durga, Sana-Blown away.

Then, the image of the Goddess and Sana floated up to his eyes. He concentrated, the images stabilized, drew towards each other like curtains and then laid over one another, became one, floated a moment more, then dispelled.

His eyes–Blink: Oh!

In the darkness, the wide open white of his eyes shone. His life fast forwarded across. All images, feelings, thoughts and understanding condensed into one moment like a lightning. Overwhelmed he dropped on his knees.

He saw an anxious father and a helpless mother trudging through the vagaries of life. He felt like an insecure orphan. Then he saw himself waking up to the face of the goddess. Her unblinking eyes watching over him. Then he saw himself sitting in the mosquito filled corner drawing her pictures like a child exploring his mother's face. He saw his parents sleeping wearily and him spending his last waking hours under the comforting contours of the Goddess' face, like a breastfeeding infant adoring his mother till he fell asleep. Day after day after day he grew up under that watchful smiling face. Day after day after day, that face percolated through his eyes, and dissolved into the soil of his senses. The Goddess became his definition, a frame of reference, of beauty, of love-A face that did not conform to that framework could not appeal to him. And all this happened while he was unconscious; without him coming to know. He did not go through life, life went into him and got absorbed within. He became what he lived. He was a palimpsest.

When he saw Sana, it was not the first time he saw that face. That face already existed within him. She was only the projection of the fundamental image embedded within. The moment he saw her, the Goddess came alive. It was not a voluntary choice but an immediate instinctive reaction. The instinct formed from the embedded impressions of the Goddess on his psyche in his childhood. And when he lost her, it was not merely the loss of a loved one. It was a loss that dug up the very foundations of his psyche and left it wounded, deep. When he saw his drawings being burnt and blown away, those wounds were diseased, to the extent that they could never be healed. Over time the wounds putrefied, secreting poison which then spread across the fabric of his temperament and made him permanently bilious and irascible. His mind was overcast with gloom like pale glasses over his eyes. He had discovered the origin of his grief. He could see the contours in the darkness.

'Now I see it!' On his soul lay a depression as if a something had been pulled out of there. Deep grooves, wounded, diseased, festering, bursting and burning, the poison spreading across the soil of his soul rendering it desolate and devastated. The face of the Goddess.

'Astounding! mind is not just a collection of memories-important events which we are conscious of, but an reservoir of every moment, emotion and experience that we have been through, whether consciously or unconsciously. Space-Time does not pass. It is absorbed and settles within. Yet, can we stop them from coming in or force them out of us? Unknown to us our senses keep absorbing the life we live and dissolve it in our being. They become a part of us and we perceive through them, like looking through coloured glasses. I am, at this moment, the road that I have travelled! Entire road, all of it-conscious and the unconscious.'

It felt strange to realize that his outlook towards life, his decisions and choices which he thought he had made rationally, were in fact instinctive responses-biased by the impressions received unconsciously in the formative years of his life. As the position and motion of any planet is determined by unknown and undetermined forces in the infinite dark space, the inclinations of our consciousness are determined by the impressions held on the soil of the unconscious. He loved Sana because her face resembled the goddess. He withheld while she stood at the threshold of his life because he was cautious, nervous-like his parents. Her sudden departure had desolated him and, in that desolation, whatever was sown had to face the scalding winds of the hot desert of his temperament. All his relations, his profession rather his entire life after that had fallen victim to this original sorrow. It was unbelievable that something that he thought he had forgotten long back, moments passed unaware, had determined the flavour of his life. You are sad for reasons you don't know!

Life depends on the choices we make but why do we make those choices? Why do we like someone and why don't we like someone else? Why are the thoughts the way they are? Why are we what we are? How far can we control it? While one can control his conscious efforts there is no way he could know the unconscious, simply because one is unconscious of them. But it is the same black soil of the unconscious upon which consciousness grows from a seed to a seedling to a tree, nurtured by the same unknown, unremembered.

As he saw he observed. As he observed he understood. His heart came down the ledge and his pulsating nerves began to settle. The smouldering embers in the grooves began to calm and the fire breathed out and finally died. The wounds dried. What remained was a trace.

A mild breeze blew over his face. He awoke into the present. He had had to travel this far down reliving all the milestones of sadness, tasting every poison again to reach the source to find that which had became the blood of his nerves, mood of his thoughts and the essence of his being. Having reached the beginning he had reached the end. That's what life is. Many answers lie before the question. Exorcised, redeemed, he looked up, looked around, got up and turned back. The gates were open. Beyond the darkness, life ran across the street in its usual clamorous cacophony.

A shadow walked out briskly and dissolved into the dazzling brightness.

Fundamental Image

If 'dukkha' or suffering is the first noble truth, as Buddha says, and desire is cause of 'dukkha' then what causes desire? Why do we want what we want? Why do we make the choices that we make and why even after getting what we choose, all that we end up with is a sour aftertaste and a baggage of unimagined consequences? On the other hand, when we restrain our desires then also, we suffer. Why are we what we are?

After returning from the hospital an irascible old Vijayant undergoes a curious transformation which lands him in a unique situation where the past and the present dissolve setting him on a journey of reflection and self-enquiry to find the answers to such fundamental questions and the origin of his grief. The answers are quite different from what he thought and what he believed.

Sourabh Chatterji was born in Lucknow, India in 1976. His essay on 'Water Wars: Implications for India' was awarded the second prize by the United Services Institution of India Journal in 2019. His Short story 'Flight' has been published in the Contemporary Literary Review, India in 2022.

Printed in Great Britain
by Amazon

61978425R10122